• The •
SICILIAN PRINCE

ADAM ANTHONY

INKWATER
PRESS

• ONE •

Dr. Brian Weinstein, Washington, D.C.'s most prominent gay psychotherapist, was trying to appear interested in his patient's ramblings. But he couldn't resist the urge to glance out his office window from time-to-time, in the hope that Shane had returned with his Porsche. *The little twink is two hours overdue,* he thought.

"So anyway, I've decided to take a sabbatical leave this coming academic year – it's been approved by the committee – in order to finish my book. Maybe then they'll finally promote me to Full Professor."

The words came from Guy Zambri, his soon-to-be-forty-years-old patient, who was sitting opposite Weinstein in the richly-paneled study/office of his red-brick Georgetown townhouse. Zambri had been coming in weekly, for about a month, in a state of midlife crisis over his work and his personal life. As he told the good doctor in previous sessions, he was stagnating at work – seemingly destined to be an Associate Professor until the end of his days. On the personal front, he had been celibate for the past year – having thrown in the towel on the local gay scene, after another disappointing affair with a young, self-centered stud – a body-builder/personal trainer named Kevin O'Hara. Brian Weinstein found himself shifting nervously in his chair when the subject of Kevin O'Hara came up, since he saw so many parallels in his relationship with Shane. Both were obviously looking for sugar-daddies, but there was a difference – Brian was extremely wealthy, and therefore it was easier for him to keep Shane around. In Guy Zambri's case, his modest faculty income didn't encourage loyalty from Kevin O'Hara and his predecessors.

"So, what's the name of your book, again?"

"*Male Nude Photography and the Classic Greek Aesthetic.*"

"Oh yes. Sounds like an appropriate topic for an Art History Professor."

"Tell that to my colleagues at GWU!"

"What's the matter, do they have a problem with it? Is it the homoerotic theme?"

"Yes and no. I've been there long enough for my colleagues to know I'm gay, and most of them don't hassle me over that – there are plenty of gay faculty around. I think it's more a professional issue – my department tends to be interested in modern/contemporary art, and for me to be fishing around in ancient Greece and in the early years of photography is considered passé to them. More and more they are into computer graphics, computer-generated art, and that kind of high-tech thing."

"What makes you think, then, that the book will get you promoted – once it's finished?"

"Well, it would meet the Arts College criteria – at least one book for consideration for Full Professor. Of course a steady stream of journal articles are also required, and I've published them regularly over the years."

"I see. So do you think it will be finished during your sabbatical leave?"

"I hope so. I'm deliberately not teaching this summer, so I have from this month, June, until June of next year to concentrate on it. And if I need more time, I'll take next summer off too. Technically, I don't have to sign a new contract until the Fall 2002 semester next year."

"Well it sounds like you have that issue under control right now. So let's turn to the issue of your current celibate status and disenchantment with the gay men you tend to become involved with."

As Guy reiterated his previous views that the local gay scene was filled with shallowness and insincerity, Brian Weinstein found his mind wandering again – back to the long-overdue Shane and the absent Porsche. *Where the hell is the little bastard?*

• TWO •

A few days later, Guy Zambri sat down at his home computer and decided to try to connect with the new internet website which had recently been heralded on television and in newspapers. The Ellis Island Records Website had established a Passenger Search database, which could locate individuals who came to America by ship during a period of several decades early in the twentieth century. Guy had long been interested in tracing his family's history, and the media blitz on this new tool finally precipitated action on his part. He entered the name of his beloved grandfather, Angelo Zambri – Nonno Angelo, and very quickly retrieved information indicating his grandfather's residence in Italy (Taormina), date of arrival in the U.S., age upon arrival, and the name of the ship (*The Sicilian Prince*), which sailed from the Port of Messina. The information appeared so quickly on his monitor screen that Guy was briefly taken aback. After a few seconds, he collected his thoughts, and fighting back tears, printed out a copy of it. He then fixed himself a cup of instant coffee and sat in his favorite reading chair, staring at the page.

Guy Zambri had never known his parents. Franco, his father, was an alcoholic wastrel who got one Maggie Ryan (also an alcoholic) pregnant. Neither

4

had any interest in marriage and settling down, and when Maggie left the hospital with her infant son, she planned to take the baby straight to an orphanage run by nuns in the Zambri-Ryan hometown of New Brunswick, New Jersey. Guy's paternal grandfather, Angelo, stopped her on the hospital steps, and after a heated argument, Maggie agreed to accept an undisclosed amount of money in exchange for handing over the baby. She also agreed to leave town and was never heard from again. Franco came and went during his son's first year of life, dying about fourteen months later, in the men's room of a seedy saloon — with a needle in his arm and a high blood-alcohol content.

During the years that Guy was growing up, his repeated and pointed questions eventually led to his learning these meager facts about his parents, bit-by-bit, from his grandparents, who were clearly very reluctant to discuss these matters. After Maggie surrendered him, Angelo and Rosa Zambri took Guy into their apartment over the small corner grocery store they owned in the Italian section of New Brunswick, and he experienced a wonderful childhood, helping out in the store from an early age, and feeling very loved and wanted. It was only when Rosa died in her early fifties of breast cancer that he began to miss having a mother. And when his beloved Nonno Angelo died while Guy was a twenty year-old college sophomore at Rutgers, he knew for the first time how it felt to be truly alone in the world and have no one. He vowed he would one day try to research his family's history, but college and then graduate school and a hectic university teaching career resulted in his putting off the task. Now, he had in his hands the best clues ever. Nonno Angelo came from Taormina in Sicily. How ironic, Guy thought. One of the main characters in the book he was writing was the German Baron Wilhelm von Gloeden – one of the earliest photographers of male nudes in classical poses. And von Gloeden spent most of his adult working life in Taormina – actually putting it on the map for scores of British, German and American tourists, in particular!

Guy pulled his *World Atlas* from the shelf and looked up the Sicilian towns of Taormina and Messina – the port from which Nonno Angelo's ship, *The Sicilian Prince*, had sailed. The towns did not appear to be far from one another, with Messina directly across from the tip of the Italian mainland. What a great start, he thought. But how to proceed next, since the papers he inherited after his grandfather's death contained very little family information?

• THREE •

When Guy dropped by his Departmental office at GWU to check his campus mail the next day, he encountered Will Davis, his Department Chairman, at the cabinet which held the small pigeon holes used for faculty mail.

"How are things going with the book?" Davis asked.

"Okay – coming along."

"You sure you'll be finished by the end of your sabbatical?"

"I certainly hope so!"

"You know, Guy, it's crucial you get the book out promptly. There's hardly anyone left on the Department faculty who is sympathetic to the subject matter, nowadays. And they all will have input into the promotion process."

Davis' comment reminded Guy of the passing of the "old guard" – faculty who had sparked his interest in Greek and Roman classical art while he was still a graduate student at GWU many years ago, but who had since died or retired. Even Davis was once among them, but he turned out to be a career opportunist who decided some time ago which way the wind was blowing among the major foundations which support research and publications in art history, and had switched to more contemporary interests.

"Well, Will, I can only hope that once it's out, they will see it as a continuum of the work I've published over the years in art journals. I don't know what more I can do, do you?"

At that, Davis pulled Guy aside, out of earshot of the Department Secretary and her part-time file-clerk.

"There's a possibility – this is strictly hush-hush, that I may wind up in the Dean's Office by the time you come back from your leave. I would then have no direct input into Departmental decisions – although I would be involved when your application materials left the Department and came to the next level at the Dean's Office."

"I see. Well, I wish you luck."

"Nothing's decided yet, and I do need you to keep this under wraps in the meantime. I mention it because you need to know that time is of the essence, since a strong Departmental recommendation is the best foundation in the whole promotion process."

"Thanks for alerting me, Will. I'll try not to disappoint you."

A few minutes later, Guy was in the English Department, finalizing plans for his upcoming trip to New York City with his long-time buddy, Chad Fleming. Chad was a gay English Literature Professor and Guy's most simpatico buddy at GWU. For some reason, there had never been a sexual attraction between them – and Guy often thought the lack thereof was probably why their friendship had lasted so long.

"Are we all set for Monday?" Chad asked.

"Yes. I'll meet you at the TV studio on Sixth Avenue at 10 AM."

Chad had obtained two tickets to a taping of the popular *Here and Beyond* television show, starring renown psychic Martin Francis – who claimed to pass messages between the living and the dead. The tickets took months of patience and persistence to obtain, and Chad was delighted to share them with his best buddy at GWU. For his part, Guy wasn't overly enthusiastic about the show, although he'd seen it a couple times. He was pretty much an agnostic when it came to speculation about an afterlife, but it sounded like a lark, being part of a live taping, and so he agreed to go. However, Guy was going up on Saturday – on his own, so he would have a weekend in New York before Chad arrived Monday on the early morning Metroliner from D.C. After the show, they would return home Monday night together.

Guy had told Chad he wanted to spend the weekend visiting several museum exhibits, but his real interest was in going to the Gaiety Theater near Times Square – the funky male burlesque showcase he discovered during his last year as an undergraduate at Rutgers – when he was first coming to grips with his sexuality. In those days, the place was a lot wilder – with rumors of dancers having furtive sex with patrons in dark corners. In fact, Guy once came across a book of paintings by a gay artist, since deceased from AIDS, which included views of the dancers on stage, as well as engaged in offstage sexual activity. The book's text described the small, seedy theater as a temple where the dancers were adored as young gods by the largely middle-aged men who sat in the audience and cheered them on.

In those early years, it was easy to cover one's lap with one's coat or a sweater and masturbate during the performance. However, when Mayor Rudy Giuliani decided to clean up Times Square, the Gaiety staff promptly posted signs saying *No Sexual*

Activity of Any Kind all over the place, and guards wearing t-shirts with *Security* emblazoned on them constantly roamed the theater watching the patrons. Guy hadn't fully realized the implications of these changes the first time he went back to the Gaiety after the Giuliani Era began, and was interrupted by one of the security men who said, "Sir, I have to ask you to stop what you are doing."

Guy quickly brought his hands out from under his coat and sat up in his seat – embarrassed when a couple of young smart-asses in the row in front of him – having obviously heard the guard's remark – started to giggle loudly.

The Martin Francis trip would offer a welcome chance to get in the Marathon Show on Saturday night, when at least a dozen different dancers were featured (some were the stars of the current show and some were to appear in the new show which changed on Mondays). He could also go back on Sunday and see the last performance of the members of the outgoing cast. At the least, even if he only saw the Marathon Show, Guy knew he'd have enough jerk-off fantasies to last for quite awhile.

• FOUR •

On the morning of the TV show taping, Guy decided to walk to the studio on Sixth Avenue from the
Westside YMCA on West 63rd, where he always stayed
when in The City, because its small, clean rooms were
very inexpensive and the building was centrally located in Manhattan. He felt great! Saturday night he
saw the Marathon Show at the Gaiety, and returned
again on Sunday night for the regular show. His af-
ternoons were spent at several art museums, checking out the new exhibits and favorite works of which
he never tired.

The lads at the Gaiety were the usual mixed lot –
but what most of them had in common was body
piercing and tattoos, neither of which appealed much
to Guy, but which had apparently become the rage
among both sexes in recent years. Body shaving –
including the pubic area, was also apparently popular, and only a couple of the dancers were sprouting a
bush. Still, the thrill of seeing each one come out in
some form of costume, partially strip, disappear, and
then emerge in a few minutes from the silver Mylar
curtain – totally nude and erect, was as exciting as it
was on his first visit so many years before. Each dancer
strutted his stuff and teased the audience, while loud
disco and rock music blasted away. As a personal

mind-game, Guy tried to recite the names of all the dancers he'd seen this weekend – Jason, Tristan, Sebastian, Jake, Orlando, Wrench...., as he walked toward Sixth Avenue.

Guy wasn't in line in front of the TV studio very long before Chad came rushing up. They no sooner greeted each other when a staff-member for Martin Francis started handing out forms for the audience to read – in preparation for signing once they got inside. The forms contained pages of legalese, but basically indicated the participants were willing to be televised, "read" by Martin Francis if someone "came through" for them, have their images used in any way (including advertising) by the producers, were willing to grant follow-up interviews in their homes, and were willing to relieve Martin Francis and his producers of any future liability due to mental distress and other unforeseen consequences of the experience.

Once inside, Guy and Chad quickly signed the forms and turned them in. The group was then ushered into a large studio and placed on bleachers. They were told the taping would be done in two three-hour sessions. The room would be very cold, because Martin Francis "reads" better with the air conditioning on high. Thus, they were advised to keep a sweater or jacket handy. They were also told that bathroom breaks would be disruptive, so they should go now, before the first session, or between sessions. One of the production assistants pointed to a table of refreshments, piled with high-calorie, high-sodium junk food and drinks. Guy and Chad decided to pass on it, realizing the snacks would just make them want to drink more liquids, and then have to go to the bathroom, perhaps at inconvenient times.

As the production assistants gave more and more instructions to the audience, and as the time for taping approached, Guy could feel excitement and anticipation in the air. People desperate for a reading came with rosary beads, pictures, and all manner of momentos – hoping they would increase their chances of being selected. Finally, the announcer said, "Ladies and gentlemen, Martin Francis!", and the lights came up and out of the shadows stepped a preppy-looking, clean-cut man in his mid-thirties.

Martin Francis stared into space for a few seconds, and then turned toward a section of the audience to Guy's right. "I think I'm over here," he said, pointing toward that section of the audience. "Does someone have a mother-figure who died in the sixth month – June, or on the sixth of a month?" Several hands timidly were raised, and the psychic was off and running.

The next three hours passed with readings for four different individuals and family groups. Guy watched the proceedings in a bemused state, but Chad was all caught up in the moment, murmuring in admiration (with most of the others) whenever Martin Francis relayed Aunt Hester's love of the color blue to her astonished relatives, and similar bits of information from beyond the grave.

After the half-hour break between taping sessions, during which time Guy and Chad felt compelled to eat and drink something from the unappetizing refreshments table – out of sheer hunger and thirst, the taping began again.

Martin Francis pointed toward Guy's section for the first time, and said, "I have an older male – father, grandfather, coming through over here." No one responded. Guy sat motionless, sensing a mixture of fear, confusion and excitement on his part. Then Martin Francis said, "Was anyone in the grocery business? He's telling me to mention the corner grocery store."

At that, Guy found himself raising his hand, but feeling as if someone else were controlling the movement of his arm.

"Does this make any sense to you?" Martin Francis asked him.

"My father and grandfather are both dead – but my grandfather was the one who had a small neighborhood grocery store."

"I'm with you – this is for you. He's showing me a statue of an angel. Does that mean anything to you?"

"His name was Angelo."

"This is definitely for you! He's showing me a deck of playing cards. Why is he doing that?"

Guy shrugged his shoulders and shook his head from side-to-side.

Martin Francis frowned, thought a bit, and then burst into a broad smile. "There's something about these cards – but I can't say more than that on TV."

At that, Guy finally made the connection, and nervously laughed – "Yes, I understand, but let's drop it."

"But you do know what he means?"

"Yes, I know what he means."

After Nonno Angelo died, Guy found a pack of playing cards secreted in the back of his underwear drawer. The design on the cards was that of cheesecake poses by scantily-clad young women. The poses were typical of their time – probably the 1940s, and nothing that didn't regularly appear in men's magazines such as *Esquire*, but Guy realized that Nonno Angelo's generation would have viewed them as risqué and kept them hidden. Having spent the past two nights masturbating to the fantasies of the Gaiety dancers, Guy found himself momentarily thinking that they might have served the same purpose for his grandfather, after his grandmother had died. However, before he could develop that thought, Martin Francis was asking him, "Are you going on a trip soon?"

"No – not that I know of."

"Hum – he's showing me a map of – I think it's Italy. He's pointing to it."

"No, I've never been there, and have no plans for travel."

Martin Francis frowned, and stared into space for awhile, and then he said, "He's very adamant about your going to the 'old country'. Was he from there?"

"Yes. Actually, he was from Sicily."

"He wants you to go there for some reason. Uh, oh – he's pulling back. He's showing white roses – that usually means they're sending their love and protection. Just know he is okay and is watching out for you. Were you close?"

"He raised me in the absence of my parents."

"Just know he is still watching out for you."

Guy really didn't hear the subsequent readings during the remainder of the taping session. He was dealing with conflicted feelings about these messages – and others Martin Francis had relayed, including knowledge of Nonno Angelo's cause of death (congestive heart failure), and the fact that his store's telephone number ended in 3333.

He realized Martin Francis had said enough to make him question his skepticism. And yet, if it were all true, what did it mean, and what was he supposed to do about it?

• FIVE •

All the way back to D.C. on the train, Chad harped about Martin Francis' messages for Guy – especially the one urging him to travel to Italy. Guy tried to change the subject – not because he wasn't fascinated and interested, but because the reading had exhausted him.

By the time he awoke the next morning, he was giving serious thought to the idea, and had just about talked himself out of it on the grounds that he needed to concentrate on his book – when he saw a happy compromise. Since Wilhelm von Gloeden figured prominently in his book and had spent his working years in Taormina, and since Taormina was the birthplace of Nonno Angelo and the likely starting point for locating his family history, a single trip to Taormina could allow for the gathering of information for both projects.

Once Guy had made this connection, he began to surf the internet for long-term accommodations in Taormina — at apartments, condos, villas and the like. He eventually located a one-bedroom condo (at a place called Villa Paradiso) which was available for the months of September and October. After several emails back and forth to a rental agent named Tonio Valli, he secured a reservation from September 1st through October 31st, using his Master Card number.

Chad was delighted with Guy's plans – expecting a forthcoming adventure which could be attributed to Nonno Angelo's message at the Martin Francis reading. He urged Guy to join him in speculating on what might lie ahead, but Guy was at a loss for ideas. At best, he assumed he might come across a treasure-trove of genealogical information in Taormina – possibly with his grandfather's help.

Chad was helpful, however, in putting Guy at ease over the issue of accumulated mail during his absence, since the post office refused to hold mail for more than thirty days, and forwarding all mail to Italy was impractical. Chad suggested that Guy give him a list of important mail to be forwarded to Sicily by air, and the rest – likely to be mostly junk mail or non-emergency, could accumulate until his return. Before leaving, Guy decided he would make advanced rent payments to his landlord, and overpayments to the phone, electric, gas and TV cable companies – based on previous monthly charges, thus eliminating any problems with them. His internet service provider automatically billed the monthly charge to his credit card, so that required no additional effort on his part. Chad also offered to make weekly security visits to Guy's small studio apartment to check on things there.

Al Italia airlines was able to book the flying dates Guy wanted, at a reasonable price, so his meager savings, scrimped together from the modest pay of an Associate Professor, would cover the two months in question, at home and abroad.

After the rental agent in Sicily, Tonio Valli, received Guy's reservation and security deposit, he emailed additional information, listing the address of the condo and the names of the portinari (Stefano and Irini Marconi) who lived at the Villa Paradiso and would be on concierge duty 24/7 to assist him and the other residents. Tonio Valli's telephone number and office address were also included, for any problems which the Marconis couldn't handle.

With all this behind him, Guy tried to settle down for the rest of the summer, working on his book, using the resources of the Library of Congress, Smithsonian, and the library at GWU.

As each week passed, excitement steadily mounted regarding the forthcoming trip – especially in light of his reading in New York by Martin Francis. It would be wonderful to connect once more, on some level, with Nonno Angelo, he thought. The only interruption from his concentration on the book came from the Trust Department of Nonno Angelo's bank in New Brunswick. Because Nonno Angelo felt he contributed to his son Franco's wasted life by over-indulging him, he went to extreme measures to make sure he did not do the same with his grandson, Guy. Thus, although his complete estate was left to Guy upon his death during Guy's sophomore year at Rutgers, all assets were to be managed by Trust officers until Guy's 40th birthday – at which time he would control the Trust himself. However, allowance was made for Guy to petition the Trust officers for basic living expenses while in school, for college tuition, and medical expenses. Nonno Angelo figured that by age 40, Guy would have learned how to support himself and make his way in life.

During his last two years at Rutgers, Guy was allowed to live rent-free in Nonno Angelo's apartment over the grocery store, while the latter was leased to a new proprietor. He also was allowed funds for his college tuition and student health- insurance policy. He did the same while in graduate school at GWU, while living in a tiny furnished room in the home of an elderly widow in D.C. But after he graduated and went to work at George Washington University, he did not draw on the Trust anymore.

Each year the Trustees sent Guy an annual statement which he never bothered to read in detail. Instead, he turned a copy of it over to the accountant who prepared his income taxes and filed the original away. Guy had little interest in money and material things, and continued to live modestly in his small studio apartment on Connecticut Avenue – making do on a modest teaching salary. The two months in Italy would cut into his savings significantly, but he had become very adept at budgeting over the years, so he was not unduly concerned.

As his 40th birthday in November neared, the Trust officers were requesting a meeting to discuss the transfer of authority. With the trip foremost on his mind, he wrote and told them that he'd arrange to travel to New Brunswick in early November to settle the matter, upon his return. First things first, he thought, and the data-gathering trip which lay ahead in Taormina remained his main focus during the quickly-moving summer of 2001.

· SIX ·

As Guy headed toward the baggage claim area at the Palermo Airport, he felt surprisingly refreshed, even though he hadn't slept on either the Dulles-Rome flight or the Rome-Palermo connection. He had been too excited to sleep. Now, he had to focus on gathering up his belongings and finding his driver.

Guy had initially planned to take public transportation between Palermo and Taormina. However, one day while he was having a drink with Chad in The Hearth – his favorite gay bar in Georgetown, a travel agent with whom he had a nodding acquaintance overhead him discussing this with Chad and asked, "How much luggage are you taking on this trip?"

"A couple large suitcases with two months' worth of clothes and personal items. Plus my laptop computer. Plus another bag with about a dozen reference books for the work I'll be doing over there."

"That's too much luggage to drag around on a train or bus. Why don't you hire a car service?"

Ever mindful of his budget, Guy replied, "Isn't that awfully expensive?"

"Not necessarily. It depends on the area. Plus, the saving of time and the convenience can be well worth it. Where are you going?"

"Sicily. Actually, I need to go from the Palermo Airport to Taormina."

"Travel expenses in Sicily are very reasonable – nothing compared with London, Paris, or Rome. If you'd like, I can check our computer files when I go into the office tomorrow morning and see what's available at the Palermo Airport, the cost, and so forth."

Deciding it wouldn't hurt to enquire, Guy gave the agent his name, phone number and date of arrival, and then bought him a drink. Later, Chad chided Guy that the agent was just trying to get his name and number and make a pickup, but when the agent called several days later, he had come through with a reasonable deal. And so, Guy was now loading his belongings from the conveyor belt onto several baggage carts, and heading for the Arrivals area, where he was to look for his driver – who would be holding a sign that read "Zambri".

Guy spotted the driver as soon as he came through the door from the baggage claim area. He hesitantly greeted the man in Italian, which was a combination of what his grandparents had taught him as a child and two years of classes in college – and was surprised that the driver seemed to understand him.

On the long drive to Taormina, Guy continued to converse at length with the driver (who also spoke "broken English"), and felt more confident about his ability to communicate over the next two months. Guy was thinking about how much Sicily looked like pictures he'd seen of Greece, when the driver pulled up to the address Guy had given him for the Villa Paradiso.

The Villa was a two-story, U-shaped building. An open, paved courtyard faced the street, and there were several small Italian cars parked in it at the moment. The driver unloaded Guy's belongings in front of a doorway in the West Wing of the building, above which a sign read, "Portinari". Guy no sooner paid the driver and wished him farewell, when the door opened and a man and woman came out to greet him. They turned out to be Stefano and Irini Marconi – who lived in a small studio apartment in the front of the building, and who performed concierge services at the Villa.

"You must be Mr. Zambri," Stefano Marconi said. "We've been expecting you. This is my wife, Irini."

"Yes – Mr. Valli's letter mentioned you. How do you do?" Guy was relieved to find his perceived limited fluency in Italian seemed to be working with the Marconi's too.

Mrs. Marconi handed Guy a key to his apartment, and helped her husband carry his luggage across the courtyard to the East Wing, where they all climbed an outdoor stairway to the second floor. The Marconis stopped in front of the door at the top of the stairs, and then motioned to Guy to unlock it. Guy then walked into a small combined living room-dining room, and immediately noticed the French doors at the end of the room, facing the sea.

"Oh, a sea view," he exclaimed, and ran to open them, while the grinning Marconis set down his bags. There was a small terrace with a patio table, two chairs and a chaise lounge. The view was magnificent, and Guy was enthralled – especially since the sun was just starting to set.

"You have a similar view in the bedroom, Sir. Come see." With that, Irini Marconi led him into a nearby room which had a large picture window facing the water.

"It's just wonderful," Guy exclaimed. "Small, but wonderful."

Stefano Marconi then led Guy into the kitchen and showed him how to operate the stove and refrigerator. Then he took him into the bathroom where he was especially interested in illustrating how to use the hand-held shower head, on a flexible cable, because American's tended to have trouble mastering it, in his experience.

Before leaving, Mrs. Marconi explained which days of the week she would be bringing him fresh linens, and she also turned on the television, which by chance was set to CNN at the moment. There was a printed list of the available channels next to the set, and Guy was relieved to see that he'd be able to get news from CNN and the BBC – as well as Italian television.

Lastly, the Marconis showed Guy how to use the telephone, and they explained to him that all charges would appear on a bill which would be delivered to him at the end of each month of his visit. With that, they wished him a happy stay, and requested he always contact them first, if he had a problem – as the rental agent, Mr. Valli, was very busy and should only be contacted in extreme cases.

After they had left, Guy prepared himself some coffee, using the small bag of ground coffee he found in the complimentary welcome basket of cheese, salami and bread on the kitchen counter. While it was brewing, he made a sandwich and took it out on the terrace. Tomorrow, he would go to the market and stock his refrigerator. For tonight, though, he would enjoy a couple sandwiches on the terrace, while watching his first Sicilian sunset. He was confident that this was the start of a new adventure Nonno Angelo had orchestrated from beyond the grave, with Martin Francis's help, and couldn't wait for it to shift into high gear tomorrow, after a good night's rest.

• SEVEN •

Guy's first few days in Taormina were spent locating the best local vendors (thanks to suggestions from Irini Marconi) for produce, bread, wine and other staples. He also got his laptop up and running and prepared a book-writing schedule which he hoped to religiously follow over the coming weeks.

Before he immersed himself in his book, he decided to check the local telephone directory for any possible relatives. He found only one listing under "Zambri" – "L. Zambri", with an address on Corso Umberto. His guidebook indicated the Corso was the main street for shops and other commercial enterprises in town, so he was not surprised when he sought out the address and found himself standing before a small shop, with the following painted on the window: *L. Zambri – Cartoleria/Libreria/Fotografo*.

As Guy opened the door to the shop, he heard a small, old-fashioned bell attached to the top of the door make a jingling sound. A few seconds later, a handsome, gray-haired, gray-eyed man emerged from behind a curtain at the back of the store.

"Yes? May I help you?" the man said.

Guy immediately thought there was a trace of a family resemblance, but he still wasn't sure this gentleman was a Zambri, or if so, a blood relative.

"Hello. Are you L. Zambri?"

"Yes – I'm Luca Zambri."

At that, Guy extended his hand and said, "I'm Guy Zambri, from America, and we may be related."

Luca Zambri's face lit up. "Oh? Who are your people? Where do they live in America?"

Guy pulled out the Italian baptism certificates of his grandparents, and explained that his grandfather came from Taormina. Luca asked if he had any pictures, and Guy showed him several – one of Nonno Angelo as a young man in Italy shortly before sailing to America, and one of him in middle age, with Nanna Rosa, taken in New Jersey.

Luca Zambri studied these items for a few moments and said, "Wait here. Look around the shop if you like."

After he disappeared behind the curtain, Guy made a cursory inspection of the souvenirs and guidebooks on display, as well as the postcards, piles of photographic film and other items in what was apparently a combination card shop, bookstore and photo shop.

Luca Zambri excitedly returned with a shoe box in hand. He thumbed through its contents for a while, and then said, "Aha! Here it is!" With that, he pulled out an old photo of two young men. One of them was unfamiliar to Guy, but the other man was definitely Nonno Angelo, dressed exactly as he was in the picture Guy had brought from America.

"This is my grandfather, Rocco Zambri," Luca said. "And this is obviously your grandfather, Angelo. They were brothers. I remember Nonno Rocco telling me he had a brother, Angelo, who went to America and whom he never saw again."

"Then we are related!" Guy exclaimed.

"Yes – yes. We are cousins – several times removed, but still cousins." At that, Luca came forward and embraced Guy in the unselfconscious manner common among Latin men.

"Come," Luca said, "You must tell me all about yourself and what you are doing in Taormina. I was just about to go upstairs for lunch anyway."

At that, Luca hung the "Closed" sign on the shop's front door, locked it, and ushered Guy through the curtain and up the narrow staircase to the small apartment above the shop which apparently served as his living quarters. As they went up the stairs, Luca shouted, "Theresa, Theresa – we have company. A relative from America!"

A short, middle-aged woman wearing an apron appeared at the top of the stairs. She blushed as Guy extended his hand. "Welcome, Sir."

"He's not a 'Sir', Theresa – he's my cousin!" Luca said, with a laugh.

Guy was directed to a chair beside the kitchen table while Theresa Zambri scurried around adding more items to the simple lunch she had originally prepared for her family.

Just as Guy was about to tell Luca and Theresa about the American branch of the family, two very beautiful, teenaged young men, with gray eyes like Luca, came up the stairs. It was obvious they were identical twins. They greeted each parent with a light peck on the cheek, and then stared at the stranger.

"These are our twins – Mario and Dario – on their lunch break from school," Luca said proudly. "This is your cousin, Guy Zambri, from America."

After handshakes were exchanged between the twins and Guy, everyone settled down around the table and eagerly compared notes about the family, as they ate and drank. Guy told them about his grandparents: how Nonno Angelo came to America with very little money, but worked hard and saved as much as he could – getting married at the relatively-late age of thirty-three, to a newly-arrived Italian girl of eighteen. He told them of Franco, their only child and Guy's father, and his unfortunate life. Guy also briefly mentioned his mother. Luca was impressed when Guy told him that at the time of Nonno Angelo's death, he owned two buildings – one with the grocery store and an apartment above – like Luca's establishment on the Corso, and a four-unit apartment building several blocks away.

Theresa asked, "Are you married?", and when Guy said "No," she replied, "We'll have to find you a nice Sicilian wife while you are here in Taormina." Now it was Guy's turn to blush.

"It is amazing how similar our life-stories are," Luca said. "I was also raised by my grandfather, Rocco Zambri – Angelo's brother, because my father died fighting in World War Two."

"That is amazing," Guy replied. "I could find very little family history among Nonno Angelo's papers when he died, so I decided to come to Taormina, in part to search local records."

"Ah – well, in Italy such records tend to be found in the local parish churches, because the country was carved up for centuries by foreign invaders, so there was no strong record-keeping central government. Our family church was pastored by an uncooperative old priest who died several years ago. When he was in charge, he made little effort to assist in genealogy searches – even with bribes of wine and food. I couldn't get beyond the year 1850 with him, because the parish records were in such disarray. However, I'll see you get photocopies of what I have collected, so you can take them back to America. The new parish priest, a much younger man, is more cooperative with such efforts, and has been dusting off old records and trying to order them for use by interested parties such as ourselves. You may get some help from him. How long are you here for?"

"Until the end of October – I have a two-month lease on a condo at Villa Paradiso."

"Okay – I'll try to set something up with the new pastor so you can get more information before you leave."

After lunch, the twins returned to school, where they were in their final year, and Theresa cleared the table and started to wash the dishes. Luca and Guy went back downstairs to the shop, where Luca removed the "Closed" sign and unlocked the front door. He then pulled out the shoe box he'd retrieved earlier and went through it again, until he found another old picture. "This is the family patriarch, Amadeo Zambri – our great-grandfather. He was the father of Rocco and Angelo."

"I see the resemblance," Guy said.

"I have a darkroom in the back – I'll see you get copies of all the old family photos I have, before you leave."

"Thanks, Luca. Why don't I leave the documents and photos I brought with me so you can make copies for yourself?"

"That would be fine. By the way, have you seen much of Taormina yet?"

"No – just a few shops since I arrived earlier in the week."

"Well, I must give you the local historical tour. It will take almost a full day, even though the town is relatively small. I could get the twins to watch the store on Saturday when they are off from school. Would that be okay? I'll come by the Villa Paradiso around nine in the morning?"

"That would be terrific. I should go now. I've taken enough of your time. I'll see you Saturday morning."

"Fine. By the way, what was your other reason for coming to Taormina?"

"Other reason?"

"You said you came 'in part' to search the family history."

"Oh, yes. In my job as an art history teacher, which I mentioned during lunch, I'm writing a book on male nude photography – especially that with classical references. So, I've come to learn more about Wilhelm von Gloeden, who devoted his life to that work, here in Taormina."

Guy noticed a bemused expression on Luca's face at the mention of von Gloeden, and before he knew it, Luca was reaching up to a high bookshelf and pulling down a copy of a small book, entitled *Classical Images*. He handed it to Guy.

"My grandfather, Rocco, used to sell postcards – in fact, that's the origin of this shop of mine, but I'll save that story for another day. Anyway, these images are from those postcards, and I had them bound into this little book. It has been a best-seller for us, among the tourists, for several decades."

Guy started to peruse the slim volume, but Luca said, "Take it – it is a gift. Perhaps you can use it in some way in your work."

Guy tried to pay for the book, but Luca insisted it was a gift. After a hearty embrace, the two newly-

found cousins parted, with plans to meet on Saturday.

• EIGHT •

"You know the word 'taurus' – the bull in the zodiac?" Luca asked Guy, as he handed him a piece of the fruit he had brought on their tour of Taormina.

They were standing on a hill overlooking the town, sipping coffee from the thermos Luca had also brought, on this bright, early September Saturday morning.

"Yes, of course."

"Well, that is the derivation of the name, 'Taormina'. The early Greek explorers thought the two summits upon which this settlement lies looked like a bull's horns from the sea below – so they named it Mount Taurus. Later it was renamed 'Tauromenion', which means 'abiding place of the bull.' Of course, there were other name changes over the centuries, resulting in the current name – 'Taormina'."

"Interesting. I can understand why it has been populated for so many centuries – the view is magnificent!"

"That's the Beach of San Nicolo, below. Over there is the Isola Bella – an island resort that was once used in a James Bond film. And Reggio de Calabria is on the other side of the water."

"I'm so lucky to have such a beautiful view of the sea from my apartment at the Villa Paradiso."

"Yes, that is true. But there is so much in town to show you – shall we go?"

They got into Luca's car and made their way into town. Luca parked on a side street and suggested they walk the rest of the way – it would be much easier than fighting traffic on the narrow streets.

Luca first took Guy to the ancient Greek Theater which later had been reconstructed by the Romans, and therefore was a mixture of architectural styles. What did remain intact, however, from its earliest days, was the magnificent view of the water behind the stage area. Afterwards, they visited another Greek theater, the Odeon, a much smaller structure. Guy was breathless in the midst of such beauty, and while Luca expertly described the surroundings, he clicked away with his camera. He would certainly have many pictures to show Chad upon his return!

Luca then took him to see picturesque medieval walls and castle ruins, before their hunger for lunch led them to an outdoor café on the Corso Umberto.

"Will you be needing postage stamps?' Luca asked, as they were finishing their wine after lunch.

"Yes, I have some correspondence to send out back at my condo."

"Do you see that tower which crosses over the Corso?" Luca asked, pointing down the street.

"Yes."

"That's the Torre Del'Orologio – the clock tower. It separates the medieval section of Taormina from the classical. The post office is a few steps beyond it. Let's go."

Guy got up and followed Luca, passing under the tower, until they came to a building on the left side of the Corso. The sign on the building read "Ufficio Postale."

"Remember, you want 'francobolli' – stamps – for America," Luca said.

"Okay – I'll be right out." At that Luca laughed.

"What's so funny?" Guy asked.

"You'll be in there awhile. Postal workers are notoriously slow in Italy."

"Oh – should I do this another time?"

"No – no. Go ahead. I'm in no hurry."

It took Guy almost twenty minutes to purchase his stamps because the clerks tended to engage in long conversations with each other and familiar customers, while they slowly filled orders. When Guy finally emerged from the building, he looked at Luca and they both burst into laughter. "You are learning Italian ways," Luca said. "Quite different from the hectic pace in America, yes?"

"In America," Guy interjected, "postal workers are under such pressure to meet production quotas that they occasionally stress out and kill themselves and co-workers."

"So, I guess we Italians know, from centuries of experience, how to live – yes?"

"I guess you do!" Guy replied, as Luca steered him down the Corso and pointed out several well-known, ancient piazzas and churches. Guy had been anxious to visit the town library soon in pursuit of information for his book and Luca took him there. Guy was surprised to find that it was in the former Church of Sant Agostino – now secularized for use as a library.

Pagan elements from pre-Christian times could still be found in the area, with the help of a knowledgeable local resident, such as Luca. He showed Guy the pagan mythological decorations on the fountain in front of the Cathedral of San Nicolo. One of the figures had become an icon of the town, after the addition of some symbolism related to Mary, the mother of Christ.

"It's interesting how the Pagan and Christian traditions are so openly melded in Taormina," Guy remarked.

Luca stopped in his tracks, briefly, as if to say something in response, but apparently deciding otherwise, he just murmured, "Yes."

After a few more stops, the afternoon sun was getting the best of them and Luca suggested they pick up some cold drinks and go down the hill to the cool gardens of the Villa Comunale Duca Colonna Di Cesaro. "There is something you must see here," Luca said, excitedly. As they walked through the beautiful terraced town gardens overlooking the sea, Luca stopped abruptly, and said – "Look there!"

What Guy beheld was a bizarre Victorian '"folly" – a building deliberately built to appear in ruins, covered with creeping plants and vines. "There are more," Luca said, as he directed Guy to several other follies. "Some wealthy English lady loved visiting here and paid to have them erected, as a gift to the town. They probably reminded her of her homeland, I suppose."

"They certainly are unique," Guy said – "although a bit bizarre in the midst of all this Mediterranean beauty."

"I sometimes think," Luca offered, "that they are allegorical figures for the British tourists who love the Mediterranean in general, and Italy in particular, but who always stand out as eccentrics in our midst!"

With that, the two cousins climbed back up the hill to the Corso, laughing much of the way as Luca mimicked British tourists and their eccentricities. After awhile they reached Luca's car on the side street which was close by Taxi Square – the little park where cabs congregated, and people met, for various purposes, on the benches under the trees.

Guy insisted that he walk back to the Villa Paradiso, since it was such a lovely day, and so they hugged and separated, with Luca taking Guy's roll of film with him to develop in his shop, later. Guy promised to call Luca in a few days, when he got caught up on his writing schedule and was free to go over for dinner with Luca's family.

Guy's walk back to his condo was light-hearted. It had been such a wonderful day – a day in paradise! He had no way of knowing that his world-view would be totally changed within the next few days.

• NINE •

Guy leaned back in the chair he was sitting in at the end of his dining room table. His neck was stiff, and he massaged it. He had been working on his book since right after breakfast, and was exhausted. He hadn't even stopped for lunch. He glanced at the battery-operated combination clock-calendar a former student had given him some years ago. It read, "3:15 PM, 11 SEP 01".

Most of the morning had been spent writing long-hand on legal paper, as was his custom. Then, after a bathroom break and some strong coffee, he sat back down and typed everything he had written on his laptop. Now he saved it to a diskette and decided it was time for a late lunch.

He made himself a large tossed salad, to which he added chunks of salami and cheese (he was so hungry by now!), and put it on a tray with a hunk of crusty Sicilian bread, and a glass of wine (he was starting to like the local use of wine with almost every meal).

He then set the tray down on the coffee table in front of the couch and clicked the TV on via the remote device. CNN came on, and he immediately saw images of burning skyscrapers. The reporters and TV anchors were excitedly passing information back and forth, with their images inter-cut with shots of what appeared to be two different buildings, each with black smoke billowing out of the upper floors.

Guy leaned forward, trying to make sense of what he was looking at. Soon it became apparent that the images were from New York City – the World Trade Center, to be exact. As incredible as it seemed, two large commercial jets, with passengers, had plowed into them within the past half hour!

TV reporters were reiterating that the North Tower crash occurred at 8:46 AM New York time, followed by the South Tower crash at 9:03 AM. There was initial speculation that this was some kind of a bizarre aerial accident, but some reporters were already speculating terrorism, in view of an earlier attempt to blow up the WTC by Middle-Eastern extremists.

The bread in Guy's hand fell to the floor, as the enormity of this horror set in. He sat mesmerized, as further reports indicated another plane had crashed into the Pentagon in Washington, D. C., and a fourth had crashed southeast of Pittsburgh. A passenger on the latter plane had called for help on a cell phone and implied the passengers were going to try to stop the hijackers at all costs.

Shortly thereafter, the South Tower collapsed, sending smoke across Manhattan. People were seen jumping to their deaths just beforehand. Within twenty-five minutes, the North Tower also collapsed. Dust and debris were everywhere. Dead and wounded were lying in the street or buried under rubble. As news reports continued for the rest of the day, reports of thousands dead or missing continued. Many firefighters were among those believed lost.

During the rest of the day and into the middle of the night, Guy sat in stunned silence, watching the endless coverage on all channels. His salad wilted, and went uneaten – eventually to be thrown into the trash can on one of his many trips to the kitchen to refill his wine glass, or to the bathroom to urinate.

Luca called around dinnertime to see if he were okay. He sensed Guy wasn't very coherent, and wanted to come right over, but Guy insisted he needed to be alone. Luca only relented when Guy said he could come by the next day, at lunchtime, to drop off some of Theresa's homemade soup.

President Bush finally appeared on TV around 2:30 AM, Italian time, to assure the American people that he would hunt down the terrorists behind these horrific attacks on civilians. After that, Guy dragged himself to bed. The wine caused him to go under quickly. He woke in the late morning and turned on CNN again, where the previous day's events were being replayed, along with updates on the suspects, how they accomplished this madness, reaction from around the world, images of lines of people in New York carrying pictures of missing loved ones, and crying — as well as images of rescue operations

Around noon, Luca knocked on Guy's door. When Guy opened it, Luca was shocked at what he saw. "My God, cousin – you look terrible." He rushed into the kitchen and placed the container of soup he was carrying on the counter. He noticed the rotting salad in the trash can and the salad bowl, coffee cup and wine glass – all unwashed – in the sink. He turned to Guy, who stood before him – unshaven, red-eyed, barefoot, and in crumpled pajamas.

"Are you okay?" he asked.

Guy gestured feebly, started to speak, and then collapsed on the couch. He buried his face in his hands and sobbed. Luca sat down beside him and put his arms around him. For a while, he gently rocked Guy. At some point, Guy became conscious of Luca's strong upper body. In his grief, he still found himself thinking about the fabulous shape his sixty year-old cousin was in. Except for Luca's gray hair, one would never guess he was twenty years older than Guy. His face was smooth and virtually unlined, and he appeared to be the picture of good health.

When Guy could speak, he uttered a string of obscenities against the "crazy, rotten, fanatical bastards who did this!" He told Luca he was glad that he alternated between agnosticism and atheism in his adult life, because he could never be a party to such religiously-inspired political terrorism.

"My life will never be the same, Luca. I'll never feel secure again, not even in my own home. I'll never look at the world again as anything other than a hostile place."

"I know what happened in New York and the other places was horrible, Guy – but you must pull yourself together. Perhaps these will be isolated incidents."

"Isolated? Ha! These people are everywhere, and the next time they may use nuclear weapons!"

"But such weapons would destroy them too – perhaps all of mankind. Do you think they would be so foolish?"

"They don't care. Hell, it looks like several dozen were involved in this action, and they willingly went to their deaths, assured of 'heavenly' rewards. They don't value life. They don't value the earth or its inhabitants!"

Luca was at a loss for words. His cousin did have a point. In desperation he tried to change the subject. "Let me get you some of Theresa's chicken soup. I don't believe you have eaten."

Guy shrugged his shoulders, indicating disinterest, but he did not attempt to stop Luca from going into the kitchen and heating up the soup. Within a few minutes, he brought it back to Guy on a tray, along with some of the bread he found on the counter. "Here, eat. You'll feel better."

Guy laughed a small laugh. "The Italian solution to everything – food. I remember when I was a kid and feeling bad – Nonna Rosa would........" He started eating the vegetable-laden chicken soup before he could finish his thought, and didn't stop until the bowl was empty.

"You want more?" Luca asked.

"No, thanks. It was delicious. I'll have the rest tonight."

After Luca put the rest of the soup in the refrigerator, he returned to the living room and sat beside Guy on the couch. "The television news is making much of the fact that this attack is the first by foreigners on the American mainland in many, many years," he said.

"That makes it particularly scary. We are now as vulnerable as refugees in Third World countries. It's obvious."

"Please don't think I am making light of this horror, but humanity has lived since the beginning of time in the face of imminent destruction, hasn't it?"

"How do you mean?"

"Well, there has always been someone stronger, more vicious and rapacious — just over the hill, ready to swoop down on peace-loving neighbors, throughout recorded history. Long before the doomsday scenario of nuclear war, the most innocent of persons has had to be prepared for annihilation at any moment. Take Taormina, for instance. You come here and see a beautiful tourist haven by the sea. But what of the people who settled here over the centuries? Did they ever enjoy real security? Taorminians have repeatedly been tortured, raped, robbed, enslaved, or killed by one invader after another – Greeks, Romans, Byzantines, Normans, Saracens, Spanish, French. And you know what? Some of them survived. *Our* ancestors survived. The Zambris survived, despite it all. You, we, have in our blood the stock of survivors in this beautiful and violent land – survivors who withstood the invasions. Actually, our ancestors were likely among the invaders, at some point in history. What I'm trying to say is that short of total annihilation of the planet by a meteorite, nuclear war, or environmental catastrophe, life will go on – even in America, even after yesterday's events. We who walk the earth today are the descendants of history's survivors, and we have to hope our descendants will also survive – although there are no guarantees. Do I make sense?"

Guy nodded, slowly. "Yes. But it is one thing to accept your argument in my head. It is altogether another thing to accept it in my heart."

"Come," Luca said. "Come out to the terrace." He took Guy by the hand and led him to the terrace. "Look to the right, as far as you can see. In the far distance is Mount Etna. For centuries it has loomed before those of us in this part of the island. We are in awe of its beauty *and* its potential terror. Nowadays, science can give us fair warning of imminent eruptions. In the old days, that was impossible, and Sicilians lived daily with the reminder of Vesuvius and the destruction of Pompeii and Herculaneum. The ancient Greeks also brought tales of their islands, some of which also suffered volcanic cataclysm. How do people live in the shadow of potential destruction for so long? Because they *have* to! That is life, dear cousin. No certainties, no guarantees. Yes, perhaps life will never be the same again for you, after yesterday. But, welcome to the human race. Annihilation – personal, group or global, is always a possibility. But still, one gets up each day, looks for beauty in the world, looks for love in others, and tries to lead a kind and productive life. What more can one do? What more can one expect of life?"

Guy had difficulty responding. Suddenly he felt childish and self-indulgent. What Luca said made sense – but still he knew that on some level, his life would never be the same as it was less than forty-eight hours ago. "You're right, of course, Luca. Thanks for your concern."

"Look – come for dinner tonight."

"I'd love to, but I can't. I'm exhausted. I need to think about what you've said, and then go to bed early tonight. I'm sure I'll feel better in the morning."

"Then come tomorrow night. Come early – around six. The twins watch their favorite TV show in the early evening on Thursdays, so we like to eat early to accommodate them."

"Okay. Thanks."

As Luca was walking out the door, he gave Guy a short, strong embrace. "I also want to talk with you tomorrow, in private, about some family business. We can do that while the twins are watching TV and Theresa is cleaning up the dishes and making her long nightly phone call to her sister and mother in Naxos."

Guy was tempted to inquire about the "family business" to which Luca alluded, but he was too exhausted. Tomorrow night would come soon enough.

· TEN ·

Guy really wasn't up to going to Luca's for dinner the following night, but he forced himself – feeling that a refusal would be rude after all the kindnesses Luca and his family had shown him.

He could have called for a taxi, or even asked Luca to come get him – knowing the twins would jump at any chance, as most teenaged boys would, to borrow their father's car to run an errand. However, he instinctively realized he needed fresh air after several days in his apartment, staring in disbelief and sadness at the television reports from the States.

And so, he made his way by foot down the narrow streets of Taormina, finally stopping at Luca's little shop on the Corso. It was just about 6 PM, and Luca was waiting for him in the doorway. After a short greeting, he ushered Guy inside, hung the "Closed" sign on the door, and the two of them walked to the back of the shop and made their way up the narrow staircase to the apartment. The twins and Theresa were setting the table in the dining room. They all looked at Guy, and upon seeing his distressed countenance, greeted him in a subdued, but welcoming, manner.

The subdued atmosphere continued throughout the meal, although Guy occasionally forced himself to make semi-cheerful, small-talk — and when he did, the others quickly responded in kind.

As the time approached for the broadcast of the twins' favorite TV program, conversation turned to a description of the show and why Mario and Dario liked it so much. They invited Guy to join them in viewing it, but before he could respond to their invitation, Luca remarked, "I need to talk with our cousin about some family business tonight. We'll do it downstairs, in my darkroom, as I have several rolls of film to develop for customers tonight, anyway."

"Okay, Papa," one of the twins said – Guy still couldn't tell them apart – and with that, they excused themselves from the table and sat on the couch in the small living room, opposite the television. As Guy and Luca rose to go downstairs, Guy noticed that Mario and Dario sat on the couch with their arms around each other's shoulders. *Now that's a scene of open affection you won't see between two brothers — high school seniors – in America,* Guy thought.

With the twins watching TV, and Guy and Luca downstairs, Theresa rushed through her after-dinner cleanup chores, in anticipation of her favorite part of the day – her evening call to her sister and mother, who lived together in Naxos. The twins were occupied most of the time with schoolwork, soccer, and club activities – and Luca was either busy in the shop or going off to exercise at the gym, in his limited spare time. Thus, Theresa was often alone, and lonely, and these daily chats with her family were very important to her.

Meanwhile, downstairs, Guy was wondering why Luca hadn't set up his film-developing equipment and turned off the bright lights in the photographic darkroom, which was near the foot of the staircase leading up to the apartment. Instead, he had unlocked a steel file cabinet and was rummaging through it. Finally, he apparently found what he was looking for, as he pulled out a folder and set it down on the small table between the two of them. In a serious, low voice he said, "Everything I tell you now, Guy, is confidential. Yes?"

Puzzled by Luca's air of mystery, but nonetheless curious, Guy replied, "Of course."

"You have come to Taormina to gather information on von Gloeden and his work, for your book. I can tell you some interesting stories about him."

Guy's spirits rose visibly. "Oh yes?"

"First of all, as you already know, many local lads – and even some grown men – posed for the Baron. What you do not know is that our ancestors were among them."

"Our ancestors?"

"Yes. Great-grandfather Amadeo Zambri posed while very young, shortly after the Baron came to Taormina to live. Later, his sons Rocco and Angelo – our grandparents – also posed."

"Really? Nonno Angelo? It's hard to believe."

"I'm sure it is. That's why I show you this proof," Luca said, tapping the file folder as he spoke. He reached in and pulled out an old photo. "This is Amadeo, in his youth."

Guy looked at the photo of a beautiful dark-haired, dark-eyed young man – holding a fisherman's net in one hand, a lemon blossom in the other, and staring straight at the camera. His body was smooth, with a hint of developing musculature and the start of a small, dark thick pubic bush over his already-impressive young, fore-skinned penis.

"This is Amadeo?"

"Yes it is."

"He's beautiful."

"He is the patriarch."

"You said our grandfathers also posed, later on?"

"Yes. Here they are, together."

Luca handed Guy a photo of two young lads, similar in coloring and looks to Amadeo. They had small floral wreaths in their hair and stood with their arms wrapped around each other. One looked directly at the camera, the other off in the distance.

"When my Nonno Rocco first showed this to me, he said Angelo – he's the one looking away – was already thinking of leaving home and dreaming of faraway places."

Guy looked again at the picture, conscious he was checking out the boys' cocks. They were both beautiful, but in Luca's presence he had to stifle a smile at the thought that Nonno Angelo's was bigger than Rocco's.

"I have several more. Here is one of Angelo alone, and one of Rocco alone."

Guy looked at them, noticing that in both pictures, they wore exotic head-dresses, and held classical-style vases aloft.

"And," Luca said proudly, "the masterpiece," as he handed Guy the final photo in the folder.

Guy's hands trembled excitedly in recognition of the photo's theme. It was a re-staging of the famous ancient statue excavated during the Early Renaissance Period – *Laocoon and His Sons*. Laocoon, the priest, had warned the Trojans of the trick of the Greek's wooden horse, and so angered the gods that they sent sea serpents to devour him and his sons. As told in the *Aeneid*, by Virgil, the gods saw Laocoon's actions as an attempt to interfere with the fated course of events. Unlike the marble statue, where the serpents were realistically carved, in the photo flowing silk scarves were used to represent the snakes intertwined around the bodies of Amadeo (in the center, as Laocoon), and Rocco and Angelo, on either side, as his sons. All three had expressions of terror on their faces.

"This *is* magnificent!" Guy exclaimed. "I don't know what to say. Such beautiful men!"

"Yes," Luca replied. "We come from their seed, cousin. They are a part of us – even now."

Guy shivered slightly at the thought that Amadeo carried the seed of Rocco and Angelo in his generous ballsac – so clearly visible in the photo, and that they, in turn, passed it on, eventually, to their grandsons – Luca and himself.

Luca could see that Guy was overwhelmed. "Here, have some wine," he said, as he reached for a bottle and some glasses on top of the file cabinet. After he poured out the drinks, he said, "I assume you want to know how this all came about?"

"Yes, I would."

"When the Baron came here, he found a small, isolated fishing village filled with incredible poverty. However, it was also filled with citizens bred from centuries of invasion and blood-mixing, resulting in the most beautiful faces and bodies he'd ever seen in a single place. He first noticed the fishermen down on the beach. Amadeo was one of them and was approached by the Baron and invited to pose – for pay. So were other boys. Because they were so poverty-stricken, they almost always accepted. However, the

Baron knew their earnings would quickly disappear, due to their ignorance regarding the handling of money, or through the deception of others who would exploit them. So, he only paid them part of their earnings directly – for needed food, clothing, medical care. The rest was deposited in an interest-bearing models' account at a local bank, with each boy's earnings recorded in detail in the Baron's account books. The photos, which were often printed in postcard form, earned the models royalties based on the number of copies sold, as well. Of course, you have heard the rumors that select boys were invited to 'special parties' up at the Baron's villa, where they 'entertained' him and privileged visitors from abroad – mainly England and Germany?"

"Yes, I have. Is it true?"

"It is true. And, the Baron insisted the boys be well-rewarded for their 'favors'. He protected them, making sure they were not abused, or forced to do anything they did not want to – even protecting them from sometimes-arrogant royal and aristocratic visitors, if necessary. He safeguarded those earnings too."

"Did Amadeo, Rocco and Angelo ever entertain at the villa?" Guy asked.

Luca looked away. He used the time needed to compose an answer by refilling their wine glasses. "One assumes so," he eventually replied.

Guy looked over the pictures again. Who could blame a lover of male beauty from wanting to stroke these beautiful faces and thighs, he thought.

"What happened to the money?" he asked Luca.

"In Amadeo's case, he wanted nothing more than to be a lifelong fisherman, so he bought new nets and other fishing gear, initially. After he married and became a father, he and several other local men who had modeled for the Baron asked von Gloeden for help in locating a fishing boat they could purchase jointly, with their accumulated funds. Up until then, they worked on other peoples' boats."

"And did they get their boat?"

"Yes. The Baron was a master at pulling off something like that. He helped them set up their own business and thus assured their future independence. In fact, most of the people in Taormina today who are involved in commerce owe their family's rise from poverty to the middle class to the Baron's having guided one or more of their ancestors in this fashion."

"What did our grandparents do with their earnings?"

"Mine – Rocco – started a souvenir stand after tourists started coming to Taormina in droves. He was married by then and tired of fishing. He first set it up on the beach. He sold postcards, guidebooks, Sicilian knick-knacks – *and* postcards of the Baron's photos. Actually, the more-provocative poses were kept out of sight and only offered to a select clientele, who eagerly came back to Taormina, year after year. A few became so friendly with him that he identified himself in the photos. They were delighted to share this little secret, of course! When the Fascists came to power and condemned the Baron's work as 'pornography', the sales went 'underground', of course. But by then Rocco had two souvenir stands – the one on the beach and another in Taxi Square, which my father, Paolo, helped operate until he was drafted and killed in the Second World War, in 1942 – shortly after my birth. By then, the family was only selling the little book of 'acceptable' poses, which I still sell upstairs, and which I gave you the first day you visited the shop. The other photos were hidden from the fanatical black-shirted thugs, for many years. I have inherited many, and there will be time to show you more before you leave to return to America. So, my little shop is actually an outgrowth of Nonno Rocco's earnings. In fact, he was still alive when I purchased this property and expanded his operations to include photo-processing and other tourist–related services."

"And what did Nonno Angelo do with his earnings?"

"My Nonno Rocco told me they financed his brother's passage to America."

"Where he eventually owned his own grocery store and several buildings. So, the Baron was ultimately responsible for his success too – thousands of miles away!"

"It would appear so," Luca laughed – as he gathered up the photos and locked them in the file cabinet. He was glad he had chosen tonight to tell all this to Guy, as it had obviously helped to draw him away from the incredible sadness he had been experiencing since Tuesday's events. However, he knew more effort was needed to shake Guy from his depression, and he had more, much more, to tell. "Guy, I can get the twins to watch the shop on Saturday. Why don't we take a drive over to Messina so I can show you where your Nonno Angelo set sail for America? It's a nice drive and the town is interesting – we can have lunch there, too. I'll also tell you how Nonno Rocco came to tell me all this and show me these photos."

Guy was overwhelmed with the information he had received tonight about Nonno Angelo's background, but he also knew that he desired *more*. So, despite his melancholia, he eagerly replied, "Yes, let's go."

They made arrangements for Luca to pick him up around 9:30 AM on Saturday, and after declining a ride back to the Villa Paradiso, he slowly wandered the streets from the Corso to his apartment. His mind raced as he walked along. *Did Nonno Angelo "entertain" the Baron and his friends – was he one of the "favorites"? Was his marriage to Nonna Rosa a sham – a cover-up for deep desires for man-on-man love? Is this why Nonno Angelo loved me so much – more so than anyone else ever has? Is this why I'm gay?* By the time he reached the Villa Paradiso, Guy convinced himself that somewhere in all this lay the reason Nonno Angelo had spoken to him through Martin Francis, and encouraged him to come to Taormina at this time. He didn't have any way of knowing it then, but Saturday's revelations from Luca would be even *more* startling!

• ELEVEN •

Guy noticed that it was almost time for Luca to pick him up for their daytrip to Messina, so he turned off the television. Reporters from the World Trade Center were starting to imply the operation there was shifting from one of *rescuing* trapped victims to one of *recovery of dead bodies*. For his part, Guy had already accepted the fact that the passage of time since Tuesday, and the millions of tons of rubble, ruled out the possibility of finding anyone else alive.

He locked his apartment door, walked down the stairs, and crossed the courtyard. Within a minute or so after he reached the curb, Luca pulled up. "Good morning, cousin!" Luca called out.

"Good morning, Luca."

Guy settled in the passenger seat, and fastened the seat belt.

"We are going North today – Messina is to the North. I'll follow the coast as much as possible, to provide you with a beautiful view."

"Thanks."

For the first few kilometers Luca made small-talk, to which Guy occasionally nodded or briefly commented. After a while Luca asked, "Are you okay this morning? You seem upset."

Guy shifted his body in the little Italian car. "No – I'm not upset. I was just watching television when you arrived. They have apparently given up on finding anyone alive at the WTC – now it's shifting to a *recovery* effort."

"Yes – I saw that. It is a shame. But who could survive all that material falling on them? And the people who jumped first — splat! Nothing."

Guy felt a shiver down his spine at Luca's reminder that some persons had jumped from the highest floors of the Twin Towers before the smoke and flames could overcome them. "I've wondered about that a lot the past few days. Why jump to certain death? And a horrible one at that. Even before the buildings collapsed on the bodies and crushed them, the jumpers were nothing but protoplasm splattered a great distance over the ground."

Luca shifted gears, sighed, and replied, "Perhaps a final act of independence, autonomy – *I* am controlling the situation – *I* am deciding how I shall end my existence!"

Guy looked out the window at the beautiful coastline and passing scenery. He could hardly believe he was discussing such a morbid subject in this Arcadian setting. He deliberately changed the topic. "I wonder how Nonno Angelo got from Taormina to Messina in order to catch his ship when he left home."

"Ah," Luca said, "in those days transportation was difficult and expensive, so that is a good question. I would think that his passage to America must have exhausted the funds he earned from his work with the Baron."

"Is it possible the Baron arranged for him to get to Messina?"

"Yes – he may have. He most likely arranged Angelo's passage for him. As an uneducated fisherman from Taormina, I doubt Angelo would have known how to go about that. In fact, come to think of it, I wouldn't be surprised to learn one day that the Baron took him to Messina to catch his ship. When you first came to my shop, what did you tell me his ship's name was?"

"According to the Ellis Island records it was called *The Sicilian Prince*."

Luca smiled. "You have spoken so fondly of him, that I suspect he was a *prince* to you!"

Guy laughed. "Yes – a prince. He most likely saved my life. Heaven knows where I would have wound up if I had been raised by my dysfunctional parents. But getting back to the Baron — do you think he would have gone all the way to Messina to make sure Nonno Angelo got on the proper ship, on the proper date?"

"*That* would not have been an unusual gesture on the part of the Baron. He was a kind, loving man. We're on the outskirts of Messina now, so I'll wait and tell you a story at lunchtime, about a trip he took several of his models on – in order to expand their horizons."

Since they were approaching the hustle and bustle traffic of Messina, Guy sat back and kept silent – so as not to distract Luca as he made his way through the city, finally finding a parking lot where the car could be left while they went sightseeing.

As they began to walk around, Guy was struck by how "modern" Messina appeared. He asked Luca about that.

"You are very observant, my cousin. Yes – much of what you see was built after 1908, when earth-quakes shook the city and eventually razed it to the ground. Many architectural treasures were destroyed. Most of them had been built between the 15th and

17th centuries, although the town was founded by Greek settlers in classical times. One of the few major buildings which survived is the Duomo – the Cathedral, along with the Orion Fountain. The Fountain was the work of a pupil of Michaelangelo. Let us go see them now!"

After visiting the Duomo and examining the Fountain, Luca and Guy found themselves standing near the Duomo's bell tower, at noon — when its astronomical clock regularly puts on a spectacular show. Mythological and religious figures move about, while one hears sound effects such as a lion's roar and a cock crowing. Guy stood transfixed as he watched the show. He remembered feeling the same way when he first encountered music boxes and jack-in-the-box toys, as a child.

As they walked away from the Duomo Square, Guy looked up at the surrounding Peloritani Mountains which cradled the city, and then at the Ionian Sea to the East. "No wonder they rebuilt the town after the 1908 disaster," he said to Luca. "The site is wonderful, isn't it?"

"Yes it is. But I want to take you to the harbor to show you where your Nonno Angelo departed for America."

They walked down to the harbor, and Luca pointed out the area where the large ships docked and where Nonno Angelo's had probably been anchored when he boarded. "*That* is Reggio di Calabria across the water. You can take a ferry boat over there from here – across the Strait of Messina, for only a few U.S. dollars."

Guy studied the charming harbor. Finally he said, "He left a *beautiful* world when he left Sicily – for an *unknown* land."

"According to my Nonno Rocco, Angelo felt he was only leaving behind an *impoverished* world."

Guy stared at the birds flying near shore, diving for fish and looking for handouts from the fishermen. "Well, he did find a comfortable material life in America – that's for sure. Mind you, he worked very hard in his little grocery store, and he was a sympathetic, honest landlord in his dealings with his tenants."

"I'm sure," Luca said. "We all make choices in life, don't we? As it happens, I am about to present you with a choice – actually *several* choices. The *first* is, which of the harbor-side restaurants do you wish to stop at for lunch? Here, let's go down that way and decide."

They walked along the water's edge, reading the posted menus outside the restaurants, before choosing one which had an available outdoor table overlooking the water, a bit removed from the others. After they ordered, Guy said to Luca, "You said *several* choices, and the first was where we would have lunch today. What is the *second* choice you wanted to present to me?"

Luca smiled at the thought that Guy listened carefully to every nuance, despite his preoccupation with the terrorist attack on his homeland earlier in the week. "Let's wait until the waiter has brought our food, so we can have some privacy."

Guy thought Luca was being rather mysterious, and could not imagine why, but he just smiled in response and made light conversation until the food arrived.

When they were alone and had started eating, Luca asked, "Was there anything about what I told you and showed you at dinner on Thursday night that upset you?"

'You mean about my grandfather – *our* grandfathers, posing for the Baron?"

"Well, yes. But I didn't expect that to cause you much concern, in view of your interest in male nude photography. I mean, you are writing a book on the subject, aren't you?" Luca laughed.

"Yes, of course. Then I guess you are concerned over my learning that my grandfather might have 'entertained' the Baron and his friends, for tips, up at the villa."

"Yes. Did that disturb you?"

"No. Not really. I was *surprised*, not disturbed. Luca, there is something I must tell you. I am gay. So, man-on-man sex doesn't offend me or upset me."

"I see," Luca replied. "Well, in all honesty, I suspected as much."

"Are *you* upset with *me,* now?"

"Of course not. In fact, I feel more comfortable now in revealing what I planned to tell you during our trip here today. Please bear in mind that what follows is *very* confidential. After I finish my story, you will have a choice to make. Whichever choice you make, you can never talk with any 'outsider' about these matters. Is that agreed upon?"

"Yes, of course. You have aroused my curiosity and have my total attention."

"Since you have researched the life of the Baron for your book, you must know that his half-sister, Sophia Raab, lived with him in Taormina and managed the household – so he would be free to pursue his work. Yes?"

"Yes. I've come across references to Sophia in my research."

"And you probably also know of his distant relative, Wilhelm von Pluschow, who lived in Naples most of his life and also photographed nude ephebes and men."

"Yes, I do. I'm including some of von Pluschow's work in my book."

"Good. Well, all three of them died around the same time – Sophia and von Pluschow in 1930, and the Baron in early 1931. A few years later – probably the mid-1930s, two middle-aged gentlemen from Naples arrived in Taromina. They had with them the names of two local residents, who were also now middle-aged. They inquired around town and finally located them. The men from Naples introduced themselves as former models of von Pluschow, who were trying to locate other former models."

Guy was puzzled. "Why did they come to *Taormina*, looking for *Neopolitan* models?"

"I am getting to that. They explained to the locals that after von Pluschow died, his business ledgers and many of his photos, glass plates and negatives were hidden from the Fascists, who grew increasingly hostile to his work. As faithful former models, they sought to preserve their master's legacy in secret. It occurred to them that in view of the governmental suppression, there might be strength in numbers. So, they examined the ledgers and tried to identify as many of von Pluschow's models as possible."

"For what purpose?" Guy asked.

"To invite them to join a secret organization which would strive to preserve his work from total destruction under the Fascists."

"Where do the local men come into this?"

"Von Pluschow's records indicated that two young men from Taormina had modeled for him briefly, in their youth, and the Neopolitans had come to Taormina to locate them, and invite them to join their secret organization."

"And did they find the right men in Taormina?"

"Oh, yes. The local men immediately remembered going to Naples for three days, staying at von Pluschow's studio, and posing for him – for which they were *handsomely* paid."

"How did they get there?"

"That's where the Baron comes into the picture. He took them on a trip to Naples – at his expense and with their parents' permission, to view the archeological findings from classic times – especially the statues of male nudes. He also wanted them to see the Renaissance paintings on display, depicting classical themes, mythology, and so forth. His primary reason was to show them the hallowed tradition which they were helping to keep alive, by posing as they did for him. Also, since they were poor fishermen, he wanted to give them a taste of the 'big city', which for them was the thrill of a lifetime."

"I see."

"Anyway, the local men had fond memories of the time spent in Naples with the Baron and von Pluschow, but as married, middle-aged men with families, it was impractical for them to join an organization so far away. They didn't have the means or the time to attend meetings in Naples on a regular basis, but were flattered to be asked. Before departing, the Neopolitans begged them not to reveal what they had been told, because there were spies everywhere, under Mussolini. The local men agreed to be discrete. The Neopolitans left the next day and were never heard from again."

"And did they set up a secret organization to preserve von Pluschow's legacy?"

"No one in Taormina knows for sure."

"It sounds rather far-fetched, doesn't it? Almost *too* romantic!"

At this, Luca motioned to the waiter, who came over to their table. "Would you bring us two cappuccinos and some spumoni, please. That's okay with you, Guy?"

"Yes – that would be fine."

After the waiter deposited the drinks and the ice cream, Luca continued. "I'm not sure if it is far-fetched. Let me tell you *another* story. Several years later, in the late 1930s – the last season before the Second World War broke out and disrupted tourism, two old English 'queens' – from Victoria's time, came to Taormina on their annual holiday. These gentlemen had been coming regularly for about forty years. They adored the Baron's work, and collected every new photo he published during his lifetime. They also enjoyed meeting the models, and were regularly invited to the villa for entertainment – having earned a reputation for generous tipping. After the Baron and Sophia died, they continued to visit, because they had become close friends with several of the local lads, who had now grown into adulthood and were fathers – or grandfathers, in some cases. The Brits would take their former favorites out to dinner, give them gifts, and reminisce about the 'old days'. On their last visit, the subject of the Baron's legacy came up, and the queens, who were quite drunk on wine at the moment, brought up the subject of Oscar Wilde. They claimed that at that point in time, a secret society existed in London, composed of some of Wilde's former lovers – and even some of his rent-boy prostitutes. They said the group met regularly to read his works, enact scenes from his writings in costume, and then to have celebratory sex in Wilde's honor."

"No!"

"Yes. Anyway, shortly thereafter the War broke out, and years later, when it was all over and tourists slowly returned to Taormina, these two queens never came back. They were old and feeble before the War, and their local friends speculated they may have been killed in the bombing raids on London, or perhaps died of natural causes over the ensuing years."

"So, I guess you're saying that if there could be a secret organization honoring Oscar Wilde in London, then there could have been one honoring von Pluschow in Naples?"

"Yes. That is what I am saying."

Guy turned to his spumoni, which was melting in the afternoon sun. As he ate, his mind raced – and suddenly, several thoughts crystallized. "You know, Luca, these stories may not be so far-fetched after all. Have you heard of Thomas Eakins – an American painter?"

"No, I'm afraid not."

"Well, he was an American realist painter who worked in Philadelphia from the mid-1800s to the early 1900s. He was infamous for making art students draw from live nude models. He eventually was fired from his teaching position at the Pennsylvania Academy of Fine Arts for requiring *female* art students to draw from live nude *male* models."

"It sounds like he respected the honored traditions of many of Europe's greatest artists."

"Oh, he did. He did. Anyway, in recent years, publications about him have appeared which focus on his male figure drawing *and* his male nude photography. Apparently, he often took groups of male students and models out into the woods and the lakes, where they stripped and posed for his camera. They also wrestled, boxed, engaged in water sports – swimming, rowing. All these activities were either photographed or sketched. Later, some of this material was used as the basis for oil paintings he did. In several of the surviving nude photos of him, he is posed leaning on one hip, in a decidedly androgynous, classic manner. Right now there is a controversy going on in the art world. His apologists claim he was a heterosexual married man who was only expressing his belief that the human body is the most beautiful object on earth. They claim he did not also view it as an object of desire. How's that for double-talk?" Guy laughed.

Luca laughed too.

"What's interesting," Guy went on to say, "is that my gay friends in art circles in the Philadelphia area swear Eakins left behind some kind of male cult – populated by his former models and students. However, no one has yet found concrete evidence. And they certainly have tried. Believe me – I know several guys who thought the discovery of such a group would guarantee a publishable Ph.D. dissertation – but it hasn't happened yet."

"Very interesting," Luca replied. "You must show me some of this Eakins' work sometime. Perhaps you could send some photocopies after you return home?"

"Of course. I have several books on him in D.C. and I'll copy out some of the more provocative images for you."

As Guy was finishing his spumoni he said, "You know, there's a more recent example of this kind of thing, for which there is more credible evidence. Have you heard of a Japanese novelist named Yukio Mishima?"

"A *Japanese* novelist? I'm afraid not," Luca replied, with a grin.

"Well, he was a novelist who, despite being married and having a family, was enamored of the Japanese Samarai tradition – especially its homoerotic elements. He tried to resurrect the Samarai ethic of male eros and military sacrifice. I read his autobiographical novel, *Confessions of a Mask* – it's quite interesting. Anyway, he spent much time engaged in body-building activities and attracted a group of like-minded young men around him – including a number of lovers. He committed ritual suicide in protest of the Post-War changes in Japanese society, and his lover-disciple of the moment beheaded him, on prior instruction, after he disemboweled himself."

"God, how ghastly!"

"Yes – it is rather gruesome. But, at the same time, you must admit it is *very* heroic and romantic!"

"I guess so."

"Anyway, since his death in 1970, there have been persistent rumors out of Japan – especially in gay circles, that his disciples have formed a secret cult to honor his memory and live the ideals he preached."

"So, the stories about von Pluschow and Wilde don't sound so far-fetched to you after all?" Luca said.

"I guess not," Guy laughed.

"Well," Luca added, as he signaled the waiter to bring the bill, "I have quite a story for you during the ride back to Taormina. And, you will have the opportunity to make *another* choice today."

"Sounds interesting," Guy replied, as he pulled out his wallet and insisted on paying for the meal —

in compensation for the gas Luca had used to drive him around today, and in gratitude for this wonderful day which had lifted his spirits greatly.

On their way back to the parking lot, Guy window-shopped, hoping to find a suitable gift to take back to Chad, in appreciation for watching his D.C. apartment. Many of the items were tourist kitsch, featuring an ugly "symbol" of Sicily – the sun surrounded by three dismembered legs. This icon was on napkin holders, planters, salt and pepper shakers, towels, plates – everywhere. He couldn't imagine Chad having anything like this in his sleek Art Deco condo off Dupont Circle. He finally decided to hold off on the gift, recognizing that he would probably purchase something for Chad at the Rome Airport Duty-Free Shops when he changed planes on his way back home next month.

When they were back on the highway, heading South to Taormina, Luca said, "Remember I mentioned the other night that I would tell you how Nonno Rocco came to show me the Baron's pictures of himself and Angelo and Amadeo?"

"Yes."

"Well, this is the story – but it is a long one. I have to go back to the War. Italy suffered greatly in the Second World War, even though we got out of it long before Germany and Japan surrendered. There were many deaths, including my father, Paolo, who died in 1942 when I was only about a year old. My mother and grandmother *never* overcame their grief after he died. I remember them only as sad, distant figures in the house during my early childhood. Nonno Rocco provided the only warmth and security for me as a child. Not too long after the War, they both died. I believe my mother had TB and my grandmother a heart problem, but Nonno Rocco always said they died of grief over my father. Anyway, I told you I decided that my career after graduation from school would be to continue the souvenir business my grandfather had started. When I was old enough, I took over the stand in Taxi Square that my father had run before he was drafted, and Nonno Rocco handled the one at the beach. After high school, I convinced Nonno Rocco that we should move 'indoors', and add other services – including photo developing for the tourists and the locals. He agreed, and I attended a short photography course in Catania. We then pooled our savings and rented a small shop on a side street off Taxi Square, and did away with the outdoor stands. By then, Nonno Rocco's age was catching up with him and he relished getting out of the elements. We did very well for the next decade, but I dreamed of owning my own shop, and postponed marriage so I could save every penny for that purpose. When I was about thirty, I found the shop, with upstairs apartment, for sale on the Corso. I talked it over with Nonno Rocco, and we again pooled our resources. However, we discovered we were a bit short of the required down-payment. It was then, when I thought all was lost, that he brought out a tin box which he had hidden away for years. It contained the cash death benefit my mother had received from the government when my father was killed. It had always been her view that the money was my legacy from my father, and so it was never spent – not even in the harshest of times. And, it was enough to help us reach the required down-payment."

"It wasn't put in the bank, to draw interest?" Guy asked.

"No. And that gets back to the next part of the story. Italy was in a state of chaos after the War – governments rose and fell regularly, the economy was unstable – so Nonno Rocco did not trust the banks with my legacy."

"I see."

"After we were settled in the new shop and apartment, he gave me a large box one night and told me to lock it in the metal file cabinet to protect it from fire and intruders. I asked him what it was, and he showed me. It was a cache of photos taken by the Baron – including the ones I showed you of him, Angelo and Amadeo. He explained our family's involvement with the Baron, just as I explained it to you. Then he asked me something which I thought 'odd' at the time. He asked me if I appreciated the Baron's work. I told him of course I did – like all Taorminians I grew up knowing of the Baron. Plus, our family had sold the Baron's work for decades. But Nonno Rocco wanted assurance that I *truly* loved the image of the male nude. I was a bit embarrassed, as I liked girls and looked forward to marriage and fatherhood one day, but he reassured me that a man could be attracted to *both* men and women. He used himself as an example. He lovingly described the beauty of some of the photos in the box. He did it in a way that was almost 'worshipful'. I could hardly keep from being aroused by his erotic language. After I finally convinced him I shared his admiration for these photos, he swore me to secrecy and then told me the following story: in the early years after the Second World War, many of the local survivors were depressed, dispirited, and had given up hope for a better future. Almost everyone was grieving the loss of a loved one, many were sick or disabled, and the future looked bleak. It was not uncommon for these men to reminisce, when drunk on cheap wine, about the 'good old days'. In Nonno Rocco's circle of friends, the name of the Baron was frequently invoked during these times, as all these men had posed for him. In the midst of one of these sessions after the War, someone suggested that perhaps they should organize a society to perpetuate the memory of the Baron, since he not only brought joy and prosperity to their hapless young lives, but also was gaining respectability again with the collapse of Fascism. At this point, one of the men told the story of the visit in the mid-1930s by the Neopolitans who had posed for von Pluschow and were starting such a society. And someone then told the story about Wilde that the old queens from England had told them just before the start of the War. What followed was an effort among these men to collect the Baron's photos and glass plates from locals who had hidden them during the repressive times, and to start an archive – not only of the photos but also records of those who had posed, when, and so forth. The group ran into a problem when they approached the Baron's favorite model – 'the dark one'. He had inherited much of the Baron's property, and he and his family had no interest in sharing control over it with others. And so, the group decided to go 'underground', initially, because they feared legal challenges from the Baron's 'heir'. Later, however, secrecy was necessary because of the nature of the society as it evolved."

"What do you mean when you refer to the *nature* of the society?" Guy asked, listening with rapt attention.

"This is the most confidential part of what I have to tell you, cousin" Luca replied. "These men, including Nonno Rocco, formed a secret society called

the *Brotherhood of the Baron*. They limited membership to only former models of the Baron and their
male descendants. The rules which govern the Brotherhood have changed over the years, with the changing times, but *that* rule has *never* changed. The purpose of the Brotherhood is to preserve the Baron's
work, maintain an archive of his photos and records,
add photos of new members — and honor his memory
in various ways."

"Various ways?" Guy remarked, curious and
puzzled.

"Yes. By re-enacting his most famous poses, re-
telling classical myths which influenced him, and re-
cording the personal memoirs of his models. *And*, to
honor his belief that the nude male is the most beautiful *and* desirable object on earth, by engaging in ritual
man-on-man sex, as he did up at his villa."

"No!" Guy exclaimed.

"Yes," Luca answered.

Guy stared out the window for a time, and then
turned to Luca. "And does the Brotherhood *still* exist
– I mean Rocco and the other original models should
all be dead by now – it's 2001!"

"Yes, it does exist – through their male descendants."

Guy spun around and faced Luca, restrained by
the car's safety belt. "And are you a member, Luca?"

Luca smiled, slowed the car to a crawl and stared
Guy in the face. "Yes, I am. I'm actually the archivist
and historian of the group, since my knowledge of
photography makes it possible for me to develop photos we take in secret, and I can keep everything in
the relative safety of my darkroom at the shop."

They rode in silence for a few kilometers, while
Luca allowed Guy time to absorb what he had learned.

Finally, Luca said, "So, now you know the *other* choice I am offering you today."

"*Other* choice?"

"Yes. Would you like to be considered for membership in the Brotherhood? Ordinarily the application process is quite time-consuming, but I have spoken with the other leaders of the group and they are willing to expedite your application — since you only have six more weeks in Sicily. We believe it can be done quickly enough to arrange your initiation ceremony before you leave – since there is no question you are descended from Angelo and Amadeo."

"Initiation ceremony?"

"That, and many other things will be explained to you by the *next* person to whom you must speak. However, I will only refer you if you truly desire referral. You do not have to make the decision now. But you know well that time is of the essence here, so the sooner you tell me – either way – the better for us all."

Guy stared straight ahead at the road for the rest of the trip back to Taormina. This day's revelations were so much to absorb! He ultimately tried to focus on the *essentials*: he, who had worshipped the male body for as long as he could remember, and who had repeatedly sought meaningful man-on-man love, to no avail – was now being invited to join a secret society dedicated to these principles. And unlike the frivolous, hedonistic world of bathhouses, glory holes, Rehoboth Beach, Fire Island and the rest – this society had been around for decades, apparently bound by ties of blood and a common ancestral experience with Baron von Gloeden – the center of the cult. By the time Luca pulled up to Villa Paradiso to drop him off, Guy was convinced Nonno Angelo was behind all this. Guy decided the message sent through Martin Francis was meant to lead him to this time and place, to this decision. After he exited the car, he leaned into the open window and said to Luca, "Yes."

"Yes?"

"Yes – I want to join."

"Ah – good. I'll set up an appointment for you with Dr. Rossi. I'll call you later with the details. Bye."

As he drove off, Guy wondered who Dr. Rossi was, but his experience with Luca had led him to trust this caring, gentle, beautiful man — with his full head of gray hair, his gray eyes, and the body of someone twenty years younger.

• TWELVE •

Guy followed the directions Luca had given him over the phone, to find the office of Dr. Roberto Rossi – arriving at 5:30 PM, as instructed. Before he rang the doorbell, he noticed a small sign next to the door, which indicated that office hours were 9 AM-5 PM, Mondays through Fridays, and 6 PM-9 PM on Saturdays. Since this was a Wednesday evening, he feared he might have misunderstood Luca's instructions and arrived too late.

He rang the bell hesitantly, and was relieved when, after a short interval, it opened. Standing in the doorway was a rugged-looking, bald, blue-eyed man who looked to be Luca's age. He was wearing a three-piece gray suit.

"Mr. Zambri? Luca's cousin?" the gentleman asked. "I'm Dr. Rossi."

"Guy Zambri," Guy responded, extending his hand to shake the already-extended hand of his new acquaintance.

After Dr. Rossi ushered him through the empty waiting room and into his private office, Guy said, "I was afraid I misunderstood the time – the sign says your office hours end at 5 tonight."

"That's true. However, I deliberately schedule my work for the Brotherhood after regular hours, when my other patients, my nurse and my receptionist have all gone. I'm sure Luca impressed you with the need for secrecy."

"Yes – he certainly did."

"Even his twins, and my son Fredo, know nothing of the Brotherhood, despite the fact that they are all best friends – as are Luca and I."

"They aren't members?"

"Oh, no. One has to be at least twenty-one years of age to even be considered for membership. Italian law sets the minimum age of consent for consensual male sex at sixteen. *We* set it at twenty-one in the Brotherhood, in order to avoid the current legal proscriptions on sex with or between minors, photographing nude minors, and all the other related concerns among the leaders of your nation and the countries of Europe."

"I see."

"Anyway, Luca has told me that he gave you an overview of the purpose of the Brotherhood. It is *my* responsibility to discuss the medical issues *and* give you a thorough exam, take blood samples and so forth."

"I'm not quite sure I'm following this," Guy said, somewhat embarrassed.

"Well, as Luca told you, celebratory man-on-man sex is part of the Brotherhood's rituals. And I understand you have no problem with *that*."

"No – no problem. After all, I am gay."

"Yes, I know. Which is all the more reason you must be medically screened and examined."

"Is this something only gay candidates go through?"

"Not at all. *Everyone* does. However, I would expect you to be even more aware of the need for caution than some of the others might be. Yes?"

"Yes. Of course."

"All right then. First, if you join the Brotherhood, you can no longer have sex with men who are not members. If you do, you will be expected to stay celibate for a full year thereafter and take hepatitis tests, and two HIV Antibody tests at six-month intervals – before you can engage in our rituals again. You know about the six-month incubation period regarding HIV?"

"Yes."

"Good. We would also test you for other sexually-transmitted diseases. This is all to avoid the spread of disease within the Brotherhood. Now your leaving Sicily at the end of next month presents a problem when it comes to performing all the tests in time to schedule your initiation. I will draw blood samples tonight and have them tested for HIV, hepatitis and other diseases promptly – I have a friend at the laboratory. However, if you have been sexually active recently, we could miss the HIV virus because of the incubation period."

"I think I can put your mind at rest, Dr. Rossi. I have yearly HIV tests – and they have always been negative, including one done last Spring. More importantly, I've been celibate for over a year – except with my right hand."

"With your right hand?" Rossi laughed — adding, "And you will swear to that, knowing how harmful a lie would be to Luca and the others?"

"Yes, I will."

"Well then, I think that if the test results all come back from the lab as negative, from tonight's blood samples, we could feel comfortable not waiting *another* six months. Mind you, all sexual activity in the Brotherhood is strictly consensual. If you are approached by someone and do not desire to engage, just politely shake your head. He will understand and there will be no resentment, anger or jealousy. We do *demand* condoms be used for all sexual activities – and dental dams or plastic wrap where appropriate. Hepatitis can be spread by the urethra picking up fecal matter from the rectum – hence required condoms for anal sex. It can also be picked up on the tongue during rimming – thus the requirement for dental dams or plastic wrap. Of course, the bisexuals among us – like Luca and I, have to be confident our wives are monogamous and that any of our extra-marital affairs with women all involve the use of condoms. But, all the bisexual men in the Brotherhood have been repeatedly warned about that."

"This is certainly turning out to be more clinical than I first imagined. Certainly more so than in the Baron's time, I'm sure!"

"Yes it is. But times change, and they have changed greatly since the Baron's day – on the legal, social, political and clinical levels."

"Do the Brothers carry all these things around – the condoms, plastic wrap, and so forth?"

"They are provided at all Brotherhood gatherings, in ample amount. But yes, in your private engagements with the Brothers outside the meetings, you are expected to follow all these precautions. Let me finish this discussion, and then I'll give you your physical exam. Fellatio/oral sex is very popular among the Brothers – especially soixante-neuf. You know '69' surely?"

"Yes," Guy laughed.

"So is frottage, where one ejaculates by rubbing one's penis against the other's belly. Mutual masturbation tends to be preferred by the older members. The Brothers don't actually engage in much anal sex. Contrary to present-day misunderstanding, neither did the ancients whom the Baron emulated in so many ways. The classic Greeks preferred intercrural/interfemoral sex, where one ejaculates between the thighs of one's partner. Do you have any questions about any of this?"

"I guess not. I think you've covered it all!"

"Good. Now take off your clothes and stand over near that wall, for your physical."

While Guy undressed, Dr. Rossi gathered up some diagnostic tools from a large closet next to his office. When he returned, he wore rubber gloves. He first drew the required blood samples, and then checked Guy's heart, eyes, ears, skin and reflexes. He made Guy turn and cough while he checked for a hernia, and then lubricated one of his gloved fingers. "Bend over and spread your cheeks, please," he ordered. Guy obeyed, and blushed a bit at the pleasure he felt from Rossi's probing finger.

"Okay – one last thing. Pull your foreskin all the way back."

Guy did so, exposing the head of his penis.

"Move it back and forth a few times. That's it. Okay. You can get dressed."

While Guy dressed, Rossi labeled the blood vials, put his instruments in the sterilizer, and discarded his gloves. He then sat behind his desk and wrote up his notes in Guy's chart. When he saw Guy had finished dressing, he invited him to sit in the chair opposite his desk and offered him a glass of wine from a bottle he retrieved from one of the desk's drawers. As they began to drink, he said, "Everything looks fine. If the blood work all comes back negative, I shall inform the Membership Committee of your oath that you've been celibate for more than a year – along with my other medical findings. That should make you medically eligible to join us before you leave here."

"Thank you for your consideration, under these circumstances."

"My pleasure", Rossi replied. Then, looking a bit embarrassed, he added, "I must say, I was surprised to see you have a foreskin."

"Really?"

"Yes. We all have them *here* – except for rare medical problems requiring circumcision. But, I had understood circumcision was routinely forced on baby boys in America."

"It has been, traditionally. More and more parents, however, are questioning the medical necessity of such routine mutilation and pain and suffering. As far as I'm concerned, the historical roots of the procedure have less to do with hygiene or health and more to do with self-hating, superstitious cults who were so uncomfortable with their manhood and sexual desire that they had to mutilate themselves as punishment. And to make matters worse, they often shrouded it in the guise of religious belief – so as to remove the topic from rational discourse."

"I *thoroughly* agree," Dr. Rossi replied. "The medical necessity for it – and there sometimes is one, is so rare, one cannot justify its routine application. But *your* generation must have been routinely subjected to it in America. How did you escape?"

For a moment Guy couldn't speak, as he was overcome with his memory of, and love for, Nonno Angelo.

He composed himself and said, "Yes – I was scheduled to be routinely circumsized shortly after birth. However, my Nonno Angelo—who was from Taormina and had posed for the Baron, was in my mother's hospital room when the doctor came in with the consent forms for my parents to sign. Nonno Angelo was adamant that I be left intact, like all Zambri men had been for generations – including himself and my father. However, my parents were being swayed by the doctor's dire predictions regarding my future health if I were allowed to keep my foreskin – so Nonno Angelo played his trump card. You see, my parents were substance abusers, and he promised them cash if they didn't authorize the circumcision. To my everlasting relief, they took the money."

"What a story! How do you know all this?"

"That's interesting too. When I first went to junior high school and had to take showers with the other boys after gym class, it became obvious I was 'different' from most of them. They had been routinely circumcised, but some black kids who'd been bused to our school from the ghetto, and I, were the only ones with foreskins. I was teased mercilessly as a result. This went on for some time, and one day after school Nonno Angelo found me crying in my room about it and gently prodded the story out of me. It was then that he told me he was responsible for my having a foreskin, and that I should be proud of it. A Zambri family badge of honor, he called it. Believe it or not, it changed my whole perspective on the matter. I ignored the taunts in the showers after that. In fact, I secretly pitied the others who had been mutilated before they could make the decision for themselves. And you know the irony of all this? Today in America there is a rising backlash against the practice of routine circumcision, and in gay circles foreskined photographic models and porn stars are enjoying great popularity."

"As it should be. The foreskin is so beautiful, so natural. The Baron photographed it so lovingly."

For a moment Dr. Rossi and Luca stared at each other, both in temporary rapture over their foreskin fantasies. Then they both broke out in laughter. The good doctor started to rise from his chair, as he said, "I think we have accomplished all we needed to tonight. I'll pass this information on to the other members, after I get back the lab results. Do you have any other questions?"

"Actually, I do. But they're not related to these medical issues."

"That's okay."

"I assume my cousin has told you how the Zambri family came to be involved with the Baron, and how much its material success is due to his generosity and honesty?"

"Of course. Before you go on, I should tell you that Luca and I share *everything*. We have been lovers since our pre-adolescent days. There is only one time we did not share our secrets. When my father approached me about membership in the Brotherhood, and Luca's Nonno Rocco approached him, we were both forbidden to tell anyone – including each other. The process for preparing a new initiate was similar to what you have just gone through. The older male relative first tries to determine if the potential member appreciates the Baron's work. If so, he is shown some of the archival photos – including those of his ancestors who posed for the Baron. Then, if he is still not offended, he is told of the Brotherhood and invited to be considered for admission. The only difference is that in *your* case, we accelerated the process, both because of your maturity and the limited time you will be among us. Anyway, it was such a great joy for me to finally go to my initiation ceremony—after months of keeping this secret from Luca, and to find him there – being initiated at the same time. Our joy at that moment was only surpassed when we later married and were blessed with sons – twins in his case, and an only child in mine."

"I see. Well, that is part of what I wanted to ask you. I was curious how *your* family was involved with the Baron."

"My grandfather posed. He was one of the original founders of the Brotherhood – along with Luca's Nonno Rocco. He recruited my father at the proper age, and my father recruited me."

"And did your family also profit materially from your grandfather's modeling?"

"Yes, indeed. The money he earned was set aside to allow his future children to one day receive a high school education. My father's graduation, years later, led to a job as a pharmacist's assistant in a local shop. I thus grew up around medicine. My father gave me volumes of pamphlets and other pharmaceutical information the manufacturers gave the pharmacist who owned the shop – and I poured over it for hours. This led to my interest in becoming a physician. Our family doctor at the time was a middle-aged man who had no sons. He and my father were friends, because the doctor sent so much business to the shop. So, my father asked him to speak with me about medical school. He met with me several times and decided I was an excellent candidate. So, he gave me a job cleaning up around his office, and at the same time he taught me many basic procedures. He made me put all my earnings in the bank. He helped me get into college in Catania for my pre-medical training, and later helped me get into medical school in Palermo. He even loaned me money for my education, and took me in as a partner after I finished all my training. *This* practice was originally his. By the time I finished my formal education, he was in his late sixties and wanted to slow down. You asked about the Baron's influence. *My* story can also be traced back to him and the modeling payments he made to my grandfather, you see."

"Yes. It is astounding how much those modeling fees and royalties one hundred years ago contributed to the eventual prosperity of the Zambri and Rossi families."

"Not just *our* families. Believe me, *many* Taorminians owe much of their present comfort to the fact that they had a beautiful male ancestor who was willing to disrobe and pose for the Baron. And yes, perhaps even sleep with him and his friends, for tips. My son Fredo, who knows nothing of the Brotherhood yet, wishes to become a physician one day too. *He* will *also* be indebted to the past if that happens."

"I find your story, and the one Luca told me about the evolution of his and Nonno Rocco's business, to be wonderfully heart-warming."

"So do I. The Brotherhood tries to preserve this history in its archives, because there are many who would call these stories sordid – and persecute us for our attempts to retain this material and preserve this tradition."

"And so, all must be done in secret."

"All must be done in secret. Well, it is late, my friend, and I must go home to dinner. I told my wife I had to workout at the gym after the office closed tonight, and would be later than usual – but not too much later. However, I have one additional story you might enjoy. Luca told you the Brothers enjoy celebratory sex after initiation ceremonies and other events. We call it 'The Revels'. After he and I were sworn in as Brothers that fateful night, we assumed we would choose each other as partners, in what would be the first time we made love in front of others, But as the Revels began, I spotted the physician who had mentored me in my educational pursuits, sitting alone, looking very proud, but also worn from years of caring about others. His body was not in the best of shape anymore, and it was covered with white chest and leg hair, to match that on his head. I glanced at Luca, as if to say – *I owe him this respect*, and without a word, Luca understood and nodded his 'approval'. I then went and lay down beside my beloved mentor, and used my mouth, tongue, hands and lips to worship him and his naked body."

"It's a beautiful story," Guy said wistfully, as he made his way to the front door. There, he shook Dr. Rossi's hand, and went out into the cool night air – sadly realizing *he* would never be able to repay *his* mentor – Nonno Angelo.

• THIRTEEN •

A week after Guy was interviewed and examined by Dr. Rossi, he received a brief, cryptic phone call from Luca. "It's all set. I will pick you up at 7 PM on Sunday. Take a thorough shower beforehand. Arrivederci!"

For the next few days, Guy's emotions alternated between confusion and excitement. He assumed he had met all the membership requirements for the Brotherhood and was about to be initiated – but Luca had offered no details in his short message, and that was frustrating!

Luckily for him, his book offered a diversion, so he spent most of the time until Sunday evening making a concerted effort to focus on it – going out briefly, only twice, for fresh bread and vegetables at the local market. He even avoided turning on the television, fearing that the depressing news from the World Trade Center would dampen the euphoria building inside him, at the thought of the adventure which lay ahead. By the time he was picked up on Sunday evening by Luca, he could hardly contain himself – so great was his anticipation of the evening's events.

Luca and Roberto Rossi were in the front seat of Luca's car. Guy squeezed into the small back seat while brief greetings were exchanged. They had driven in silence only a few kilometers north of town, when Luca suddenly slowed down and pulled up behind two other cars which were slowly turning into a gate by the right side of the road. As the cars inched forward, Guy noticed a high stone wall and thick trees on either side of the gate, making it difficult to determine what this place was. After awhile, Guy could see a very thin man with a black "pencil" mustache standing beside the gate. He peered into each car and wrote something on a clipboard he held. When Luca's car reached him, the gentleman leaned in the window and Luca said, "Luca Zambri, Roberto Rossi, and Guy Zambri – the initiate."

"Aha," the man said to Guy. "I am your host, Pietro Stanza. Welcome and pass."

As they proceeded through the gate, Guy momentarily thought he had seen this man somewhere before, but his attention was diverted to a sign posted near the gate: *Proprieta Privata – Cascina Stanza*, which he translated as, *Private Property – Stanza Farmhouse*. They then passed two small outbuildings – each fenced in. It was still light enough outside for Guy to notice that some chickens were scratching in the ground within one of these fenced areas, and several goats were enclosed in the other.

Opposite these two buildings was a larger one – obviously the farmhouse. However, Luca passed by that too, until he came to a long, one-story building that backed up against a grove of trees. A half-dozen cars were already parked near this building and Luca parked his near theirs. As they emerged from the car and walked toward this building, Guy could observe glimpses of the sea between the trees in the nearby grove. This farm, he realized, was apparently located on the edge of a cliff overlooking the sea.

As they entered the building, they encountered a small, tiled foyer which led directly into what appeared to be a locker room. The room was long and narrow, with a wooden bench running down the center. Metal gym-style lockers lined the walls. There were several men already there, disrobing and placing their belongings in the lockers. Smiles and brief greetings were exchanged between them and Guy's companions. Luca motioned to Guy to choose a locker next to his and Roberto's. Luca and Roberto immediately started to undress, and Guy followed their actions. As Guy glanced around, trying to figure out what this place was, he couldn't help checking out the dicks which surrounded him. He smiled as he noted they were all uncut. But he was puzzled to note that each man, including Luca and Roberto, was wearing some type of gold medallion around his neck, suspended on a thin gold chain. The object was about the size of an American quarter, but he couldn't get close enough to ascertain what it depicted.

As he undressed and continued to look around the narrow room, he noticed there was apparently a shower area at the far end – opposite the entrance foyer. He could see several shower heads on one of its walls, part of the damp floor, and heard the slow drip of a faucet in need of a new washer.

His inspection of the area was brought to an abrupt halt when he realized that Luca and Roberto were sitting on the bench, patiently waiting for him to finish undressing. He blushed a bit in embarrassment, threw the last of his clothes into the locker, and joined them. As more men were arriving through the front door, he followed Luca and Roberto through another door which led to a large room – almost as big as the building itself.

The first thing that struck Guy was that the room looked like a gymnasium. The floor was almost completely covered with the kind of padded mats used for wrestling, tumbling and calisthenics. The long wall opposite was lined with exercise and body-building equipment – assorted weights, benches, a stationery bike, a treadmill. The narrow wall to his Guy's right was lined with two large wooden armoires, which had a tall plastic trash can between them. The end wall to his left appeared to have a platform abutting it. The platform was raised several feet higher than the rest of the floor, and was curtained off by drapery material suspended by a thick wire. It was obviously some kind of stage.

Luca ushered Guy to a mat near the stage and motioned for him to sit down. He did so and Luca joined him. Roberto sat on a nearby mat. A half-dozen or more men were already seated on mats – singly or in pairs. Quickly, others entered from the locker room and it wasn't long before Pietro Stanza , the thin man with the mustache, came to the front of the room. He was holding a small bell and as he rang it, Guy suddenly remembered where he had seen him before – he was a waiter at the Wunderbar on the Corso.

"Brothers," Pietro Stanza began, "we are here tonight to welcome a new Brother into our fold – all the way from America!" At this, Guy heard low murmuring throughout the room. "But first," Stanza continued, "we must honor the memory and work of our Master, the Baron. And so for your admiration and enjoyment, let the entertainment begin!"

At this, Luca, Roberto and several others jumped up and headed toward the curtain on the stage. Guy started to rise, but Luca motioned to him to stay put. After Luca and the others disappeared behind the suspended curtain, Guy could feel the excitement in the room. The audience members looked at each other and smiled in anticipation. After a short while, Pietro Stanza came forward again and stood in front of the curtain. Guy couldn't help but notice that his long, thin, body and pencil-thin mustache were matched by one of the longest, thinnest cocks he's ever seen. Stanza interrupted Guy's reverie by ringing his little bell again, and as he stepped off to the side, the curtains were parted from behind. On the small stage, lighted by numerous candles in a variety of shapes and sizes, a beautiful naked young man appeared, standing in a sensuous manner with a wreath of leaves in his hair and a bunch of grapes in one hand. The other hand was provocatively raised behind his head, as he leered at the audience. The young man did not move, but stood as still as a statue. Pietro Stanza pointed to him and said, "Behold Bacchus, the God of Wine." The audience clapped enthusiastically, as the young man held the pose for a minute or more. The curtains were then closed from behind. Guy could see the hands and feet of whoever was operating the curtains and shortly thereafter, they opened again. This time, two men who looked to be in their early thirties were standing side-by-side, holding zodiac cards which identified them as the Gemini twins. Guy gasped at their beauty. As the others applauded and cheered, he noted they had reddish-brown hair, and stunning green eyes. They were definitely brothers, but Guy wasn't sure they were twins. One appeared to be several inches taller than the other and perhaps a year or two older. They held their pose long enough for Guy to notice that the flickering candlelight on the stage allowed the red highlights of their ginger-colored pubic hair to sparkle like fire. He reached down and automatically started to stroke himself, but stopped as he remembered he was not in the privacy of his bedroom. As the curtains closed, Guy looked around and noted that several of the men in the audience were, in fact, stroking themselves openly.

Several more presentations were made, each an allusion to a classical myth or one of the typical poses appearing in the Baron's work. Guy realized that tonight's entertainment was obviously a series of "tableaux vivants" – frozen poses duplicating imagery reflective of the Baron's work and his sources of inspiration. Guy sat straight up and took special notice when the curtains again parted and Roberto Rossi stood center stage, with a lustful leer on his face. In his arms he held a twenty-something young man who was trying to look like a ephebe by having shaved his pubic area and body. The young man clung to Roberto's neck with one hand — in mock fear, and held a drinking cup in the other. Just as Guy made the connection – *Zeus and Ganymede*, Pietro Stanza announced the same to the audience – adding that Ganymede was Zeus's chosen cup-bearer. As Roberto and the "ephebe" held the pose, Guy studied their bodies. Roberto was incredibly sexy, in a Yul Brynner kind of way. His handsome bald head, pierced by bright blue eyes, surmounted a muscular, hirsute body. The thick black chest pelt and pubic bush contrasted nicely with the smooth body of "Ganymede". Guy was amazed that a man of sixty, such as Roberto, could be in such fabulous shape. After the curtains closed, Guy wondered how much more display of manly beauty he could endure before he involuntarily splattered cum all over himself. As he sat there trying to control himself, Pietro Stanza announced, "And finally.....", as the curtains parted. Everyone seemed to gasp out loud. Luca stood in the center of the stage, with an "ephebe" on either side.

The ephebes' bodies were shaved to appear younger, like that of the Ganymede model. All three figures had frozen looks of terror on their faces. Long silk scarves were intertwined among their bodies. *Laocoon and His Sons*, Guy thought, noting that the silk scares were a clever way of depicting the devouring snakes sent to Laocoon as punishment, from the Gods. Pietro Stanza verified Guy's interpretation for the audience, while Guy studied Luca's body. Like Roberto, Luca was in incredible shape for a man of sixty. His pubic hair had turned a silver shade of gray to match that on his head. His gray-colored eyes shown brightly in the handsome head which surmounted a body only sparsely covered with hair on his arms, chest and legs. The audience's response to the tableau was thunderous. After the curtains closed, Pietro Stanza opened them to reveal all those who participated in the event, and the performers took a final bow before returning to their respective mats.

After the noise subsided and everyone was seated, Stanza rang his bell again and said, "And now, Brothers, it is time to welcome a new member into our fold. Would the initiate and his sponsor please come forward?"

At this, Luca stood up, reached down and pulled Guy to his feet. He led him to the stage, where he positioned the two of them in front of the curtains, facing Stanza. Then Pietro Stanza intoned, "Who do you bring us, Brother Luca?"

"I bring you Guy Zambri."

"And does he have the proper lineage?"

"Yes, Brother. He is the grandson of Angelo and great-grandson of Amadeo – both of whom posed for the Baron."

"And has he met all the requirements for entrance into our rank?" At this point, Pietro Stanza turned toward the audience. Roberto Rossi rose from his mat and addressed Stanza. "Yes, he has, my Brother."

"Good," Stanza replied. Then to Luca he said, "Proceed."

Luca turned to Guy and, placing his hands on Guy's shoulders, said, "Do you swear to keep secret all knowledge of the Brotherhood?"

"I do."

"Do you swear you are a true descendant of the Baron's models?"

"I do."

"Do you swear you bring no known disease to your Brothers?"

"I do."

"Do you promise you will notify Brother Rossi of any changes in your medical condition or any other breach of our rules regarding sexual activity outside the Brotherhood?"

"I will."

Luca then turned to Pietro Stanza, who handed him a gold medallion on a chain. Luca placed it around Guy's neck and said, "Kiss this symbol of the secret Brotherhood, and wear it at all times."

Guy kissed the medallion and noticed that it appeared to possibly represent the zodiac sign of Taurus the Bull. This made no sense, as he was not a Taurus and couldn't believe everyone in the Brotherhood was one. Before he could contemplate that issue further, Pietro Stanza was saying to Luca, "As sponsor of this new Brother, welcome him to our fold."

At that, Luca took Guy in his arms and French-kissed him deeply, while the audience cheered. By the time Luca released him from his powerful arms, Guy's manhood was fully erect. However, he felt no embarrassment as Luca led him back to their mat. After they were seated, Pietro Stanza rang his bell again and said, "Let the Revels begin – let us rejoice in our manhood, our love for each other, and our undying admiration for the Baron and his legacy."

Almost immediately, men began to move from one mat to another. Guy was confused. Luca touched his shoulder and said, "Observe and learn. Tomorrow I shall come to your place for lunch and I shall answer *all* your questions regarding what you have seen and heard here tonight."

As Guy watched, he realized the men were pairing up for sex. In some cases, three-ways were being arranged. People started walking quickly toward the two wooden armoires along the end wall. They opened one of them and returned with condoms, lubricant and other sex-related materials and devices. Soon, the room was filled with the scent of man-musk. As Guy surveyed the activity, it became apparent that Roberto Rossi was correct when he told him, during his physical exam, that the Brothers preferred fellatio or sixty-nine. That seemed to be the most common activity in view, although the very oldest men – who looked to be in their eighties, were engaged in solitary or mutual masturbation. Only several couples were engaged in anal intercourse, and to Guy's surprise, Roberto Rossi was one of them. Roberto had gone to share the mat of a man about Guy's age, after the initiation ceremony ended. The man had a very visible twisted right foot, which made his right leg shorter than his left – causing a noticeable limp, which Guy first observed in the locker room, earlier. Now, he was on his knees, while Roberto made love to him, doggy-style, from behind.

Just as Guy was assuming this would be a night of voyeurism for him, Luca whispered in his ear, "Have you seen enough? Are you ready to join in the Revels?"

Guy looked into Luca's beautiful gray eyes and nodded.

"May I have the honor of exploring your manly body tonight?" Luca asked, with a broad grin.

"Oh yes, dear Luca. Please make love to me," Guy pleaded, as his engorged cock throbbed with anticipation. Luca smiled, got up and went over to the armoire that contained the supplies. He returned with several condoms. He stood over Guy as he covered his own erect cock with one, and then he knelt down and "dressed" Guy for love. Luca then took Guy in his arms and crushed him as he overwhelmed him with deep soul kisses, stroking his body at the same time. After awhile, Luca let go and moved into the position for soixante-neuf. Before Guy could even realize what had happened, Luca was devouring him. Automatically, Guy responded in kind, as Luca thrust his manhood into Guy's face. They immediately struck up a smooth rhythm, which ended quickly when they simultaneously ejaculated a few minutes later. Guy lay on the mat gasping for air. Luca spun around and took Guy in his arms and cradled him like a newborn babe. Guy felt so safe, so secure, with his head against the powerful chest of this sweet, beautiful man. Soon, his eyes closed, and he dozed lightly.

Later, Guy was awaken from his light slumber by a combination of shoulder shakes by Luca and Pietro Stanza's bell-ringing. Stanza was standing before the curtains, his face flushed from the sex he had just enjoyed. "And now, Brothers, prepare to welcome our new member, before cleansing yourselves."

The Brothers slowly rose from their mats, gathered up the used condoms and other material, and headed toward the trash can that was positioned between the armoires.

After depositing the refuse, they each reached into the other armoire and removed a bath towel, which was slung over their respective right shoulders. While this was occurring, Luca was guiding Guy to the door. He positioned Guy right next to it, and himself next to Guy, but away from the door. Soon, a line of towel-bearing Brothers formed and Guy realized this was to be a reception line of sorts. Pietro Stanza, who Guy later realized would have to leave first in order to unlock the gate as the Brothers departed, approached Luca first. "Congratulations, Brother, on the continued association of the honored Zambri family with the Brotherhood."

"Thank you," Luca replied. "Thank you for arranging this wonderful evening on such short notice."

"You are welcome, Brother." And then turning to Guy, Stanza said, "And welcome to you, our American Brother." With that, he gave Guy a handshake and a gentle kiss on the cheek.

One by one, the Brothers approached, first congratulating Luca, and then welcoming Guy. When Roberto reached Guy, he embraced him – pressing his pelted chest against Guy's, and giving him a French kiss which almost caused Guy's knees to buckle. Guy was still lightheaded when the two green-eyed, reddish-haired "twins" approached and welcomed him with gentle kisses on both his cheeks. Up close, they were even more beautiful, and Guy was now certain that they were not twins. One was definitely a bit older than the other.

As the men passed out of the gym, they formed a line in the locker room, waiting patiently to take a shower. Guy and Luca were the last to enter the shower room, which only had 4 operating units. The two of them stood under one showerhead and gently soaped each other's body – as the other Brothers were doing. After they rinsed off, Luca and Guy returned to the locker room. Only a handful of Brothers were still there – toweling each other off. Roberto was sitting on the bench – almost completely dressed. Guy and Luca toweled each other off, lovingly, and as they dressed, Guy noticed each departing Brother was reaching into his wallet and placing some bills in a small slotted wooden box near the door. Roberto noticed the puzzled look on Guy's face. "For Pietro." he said, adding, "He endures expenses on our behalf – upkeep on this building, laundering the towels, buying the condoms and supplies, paying the electric bill, cleaning the showers."

"Of course," Guy responded. "But how much?"

Luca and Roberto exchanged glances. "It's up to you," Luca replied. "But most deposit about 10,000 lira."

Guy thought for a moment, as he pulled on his pants. "Why that's only about $6.50 in U.S. dollars."

"Yes," Luca said.

"Well, this was a special night for me, so I'd like to leave more."

"As you wish," Roberto replied.

A few minutes later, fully dressed, they passed the box on their way out and Guy deposited 50,000 lira. At the gate he leaned out of the car window and thanked Pietro Stanza profusely for arranging the evening's events. Stanza shook his hand again and waved good-bye as the trio drove through the gate. Guy looked back and saw Pietro locking the gate for the night, behind them.

They rode in silence back to Taormina. Guy was bursting with questions, but was mindful Luca had told him he would come to his condo for lunch tomorrow and answer all of them – so he held his tongue.

As he alighted from the car in front of the Villa Paradiso, he leaned forward and lightly kissed both Luca and Roberto on the cheek. "Thank you for making me feel I have been re-born in the land of my ancestors." he whispered.

"You have been." Luca laughed. "You have been."

· FOURTEEN ·

Guy awoke around ten on the morning after his initiation into the Brotherhood of the Baron. The night before, he was so exhausted after coming home from the ceremony that he went straight to bed without even turning on the television to see the latest horrors from the World Trade Center. Sex *always* made him sleepy, and his encounter with Luca had been so intense, he was still lethargic the next day. As he was making himself a cup of coffee, he suddenly remembered Luca was coming to lunch so he could answer any questions he might have about the evening's events. Guy glanced inside the condo's small refrigerator and decided he needed to rush out for lunch items. He quickly shaved and showered and then made a brisk swing through his favorite shops, picking up prosciutto, melon, fresh bread — and cannoli, for desert.

He wasn't back at the condo very long when Luca knocked on his door. "Good afternoon, Cousin" Luca exclaimed, as he entered. Instead of the usual embrace and light kiss on the cheek, Luca grabbed Guy heartily and kissed him directly on the mouth, with probing tongue. Guy responded in kind, recognizing that after the previous night's events, their relationship had obviously reached a new level of intimacy.

After a few more hugs, they separated and Guy suggested Luca sit at the table on the terrace while he prepared lunch. When he returned from the kitchen, he brought the meat, melon, bread and a bottle of wine. "I have cannoli and coffee for later," he told Luca.

"Great. I've closed my shop for an hour, so I think we ought to get right at it. I'm sure *you* have many questions, and *I* have some things I need to discuss with you, too."

"Oh," Guy replied. "Do you want to go first?"

"No, of course not. You must be bursting with questions!"

"I am. Okay. Well first, what kind of place was that last night? I mean, I gather it's a farm owned by Pietro Stanza, but…."

"Okay. Yes, it's Pietro's. It was his father's before him. The old man was one of the founders of the Brotherhood, along with my Nonno Rocco, and he offered it to the group as a private meeting place. The fact that the property included the grove, overlooking the sea, where the Baron often took photographs, made it even more attractive to the Brothers."

"The Baron photographed there?"

"Yes."

"Was it his villa?"

"No. It wasn't his villa. But, he knew the owners of the property and paid them a fee to use it occasionally. He felt the setting was perfect for his purposes."

"I see. And how did it come into Pietro's father's hands?"

"As you can guess, his grandfather supplemented his fishing income by posing for the Baron, and that money provided the family with a nest-egg that eventually helped buy the farm."

"So we have *another* example of a present-day Taorminian who ultimately owes his current financial security to the Baron!"

Luca laughed. "Yes, indeed."

"Are there *any* locals *not* beholden to the Baron?"

"Very few. Very few."

"What about the building we were in last night? It's certainly not a typical farm structure. It's more like a fitness center or a gymnasium."

"You're right. After years of meeting in the grove and dealing with inclement weather at times or risking being seen by prying eyes, the Brothers offered to contribute funds for the building, and to build it themselves. For over a year, we spent our spare time working on it – in a rather haphazard fashion, since we all had other commitments. Luckily, there was at least one member in the Brotherhood who was trained in each of the major skills needed – carpentry, plumbing, electrical wiring – so we didn't have to involve *outsiders*. And yes, it is like a gymnasium. In fact, we call it the *palaestra*. I'm sure you know the word."

"Yes – the ancient Greek name for a wrestling court."

"Roberto put that name on it. He has been a lifelong devotee of Greco-Roman wrestling."

"Interesting."

"In addition to holding our meetings there, it is available as a fitness center for the Brothers, at all times. When Pietro is not at home, the gate to the farm is locked, but a key, secreted in the stone wall, allows us to come and go. Roberto and I try to go there once a week for exercise – and of course for love, afterwards."

Guy looked down at his plate, trying to conceal the red flush that he felt covering his face.

"Aha!" Luca laughed. "You are still a little shy about how matter-of-factly we talk of such things among ourselves."

Guy gathered his thoughts before speaking. "Obviously, as a gay man, I am no neophyte in regard to man-on-man love. It's just that I've never quite seen it presented as something so *normal*, so *free*, as I did last night."

"Surely you went to those bath-house places in America, did you not? Where there was nudity and open sex between men?"

"Actually, I only went twice — when I first 'came out'. I was repelled by the dark, dirty, furtive atmosphere the first time. A friend gave me the address of another place, which was supposed to be more 'up-scale', but I came away with the same misgivings. Luckily for me, all I did was watch – I didn't participate. This was the early '80s, after Nonno Angelo had died, and I probably saved myself from HIV-infection by quickly removing the bath-house scene from my life. Speaking of that, I have another question for you – more of a comment. It has to do with all the safe-sex measures last night. I mean, I sat through Roberto's clinical lecture when he examined me and should have expected it, but all that *ritualized* use of condoms, dental dams, and so forth. I wasn't expecting such careful attention to disease prevention in the midst of an.... *orgy* – may I use the word?"

Luca laughed. "Yes, I'm sure it looked a bit strange to see such rampant passion all around, being delayed while people donned rubber gloves, and took other precautions! But that is all due to Roberto's influence on the Brotherhood. After the sources of HIV-infection were better understood, Roberto made a crusade of protecting the Brothers. He pushed for detailed physical exams, precautions, and periodic lectures on the subject – so the newer members could be sensitized to the issue and the older ones reminded."

'Well, he certainly has instilled caution in the minds of the Brothers!"

"He has done it out of love – love for the Brothers and love for the Brotherhood – which of course would collapse, like so many small African countries one reads about, if AIDS were rampant among us."

"Thank goodness for Roberto, his expertise, and his concern!"

"Amen! Anyway, do you have other issues I can clarify?"

"Um...yes. The *medallion* I was given." At this point, Guy reached inside his shirt and pulled it out. "What does it signify? I mean, it resembles the zodiac sign for Taurus the Bull, but *my* birthday is in early November – and surely *all* the Brothers were not born between the twentieth of April and the twentieth of May!"

Luca laughed, as he finished the last of his prosciutto and melon. "You are correct – it is related to the bull. It has a *double* meaning, actually. The symbol within the circle is a representation of the forehead and horns of a bull. The *first* meaning relates to Taormina itself. Remember I told you that the earliest settlers looked up at this promontory from the beach below — where their ships had landed, and thought it looked like the horns of a bull?"

"Yes, I do. That's where the name comes from, doesn't it?"

"Correct. *Taormina* is a corruption of various names given this settlement, over the centuries. However, the root of all the names is the Greek word for *bull*."

"I see. And the *second* meaning of the medallion?"

"The other meaning refers to *us* – the Brothers. The bull is the symbol of male virility, and like the bull, we also proudly carry the life-force in our swollen testicles. We venerate the bull because we identify with him."

Guy stacked the dirty luncheon plates and pushed them to the side of the table. Then he said, "And of course the bull has been prominent in Mediterranean and Aegean rituals for centuries – among the Minoans on Crete and the Roman Centurians who were members of the Cult of Mithras, meeting in secret."

"Exactly. Even today, in Spain for instance, eating the bull's testicles is believed to enhance virility. The butcher shops slice them paper-thin and they are fed to young boys as soon as they can eat solid food, in parts of Spain."

"I wonder if Viagra will make that custom obsolete one day," Guy joked.

"Viagra? Viagra—oh yes. The pill that's been in the news. Maybe so," Luca laughed in response.

"Tell me," Guy asked, "how do the married men in the Brotherhood explain the medallion to their wives? After all, you told me last night to wear it *always*."

"Good question. Those who were born under the sign of Taurus just say it's their zodiac symbol. Others call it a 'good luck' charm. That's easy to do in Sicily – superstition abounds here and in Italy, as a whole. Some pass it off as a friendship charm or school logo. It's not been an issue."

"And where do they come from? Surely, they are custom-designed and made."

"Yes. Luckily for the Brotherhood, we have a jeweler among our members – Raphael Massi. He has a shop in the Corso – you may have passed it?"

"I don't recall. But don't tell me – his family's shop had its origins in the Baron's generosity toward one of his male ancestors!"

"You've got it, Cousin!"

At that, Guy rose and went to get the coffee and cannoli while Luca took a bathroom break. When they were seated again at the small table overlooking the sea, on this gorgeous October day, Guy continued. "I only have two more questions on my list. The body-shaving by the Brothers who posed as ephebes – Ganymede, Laocoon's sons? I assume that was to make them look more in character – younger, since no one can join who is not at least twenty-one years old?"

"Yes. In the Baron's day, one could photograph adolescents, be intimate with them, and have little fear of retribution. However, *we* live in a very different world today, so every attempt must be made to avoid criminal activity. Actually, when the Brotherhood was originally founded by my Nonno Rocco and the others after the Second World War, they allowed eighteen year-olds to join. However, in recent years, with international perspectives changing, some of the members – led by Roberto, pressed for the age requirement to be raised to twenty-one. We felt safer from unjust prosecution afterwards, but quickly noticed that the aesthetics of the photos we produced, and the entertainments we devised, no longer re-sembled the Baron's legacy. So, someone suggested all members under the age of twenty-five be required to engage in full-body shaving – in order to at least *appear* as if we had ephebes among us."

"Doesn't that raise questions in some quarters – you know, their shaved bodies are noticed by their wives, or others?"

"If there is a concern over that, an exception is made. However, most of our members marry well af-ter the age of twenty-five – like Roberto and I did, primarily in the hope of having sons who will con-tinue the Brotherhood."

"I see. My last question is related to that one, in a way. Last night the entertainment consisted of tableaux vivants. Is that always the case?"

"No. We alternate events. Sometimes we have sessions where we photograph each other in the Baron's style. Or, if we have a number of new mem-bers who are not well-versed in the Baron's work, we present lectures on him. Along that line, a popular event is for an individual to relate his family's con-nection to the Baron, and how it led to the family's present-day prosperity. Since the Brothers value healthy bodies so much, we also have body-building exhibitions, with prizes, and Greco-Roman wrestling matches – which Roberto coaches. So, there are a number of activities when we meet – with or without new initiates waiting to be sworn in."

"I regret I won't be here to see some of these other activities in the future."

"I do too. The tableaux vivants were presented last night because we could do them on short notice – the members are familiar with the basic poses and myths."

"Well, it was wonderful. What a feast of manly beauty! The way the many burning candles on the stage reflected off those naked bodies – hard, hung, unashamed, proud and beautiful!"

"Do you include mine among them?" Luca said with a laugh.

"Yes, I do" Guy responded, as he reached across the table and squeezed Luca's left hand.

"Ah," Luca replied with a slight leer on his face, "too bad I must leave for the shop shortly. Do you have any other questions? If not, I have some matters for discussion."

"No. I guess that's it."

"Okay, then. Do you have your daybook handy? I've taken the liberty to schedule some events during your remaining days here."

"Let me get it from the top of the bureau in the bedroom."

When Guy returned with the book and a pen, Luca said, "We need to photograph you for the Brotherhood's archives. Normally, we can wait awhile after the initiation to do that, but with your leaving for America at the end of the month, that must be expedited."

"I have some extra passport photos you can have, but I expect you want something else."

"Yes. All members must be photographed nude, in the style of the Baron, for our archives. We do it at Pietro's – in the grove during nice weather, or indoors on the stage – as a last resort."

"I see. When do you want to do it?"

"Roberto wants to join us – we'll bring a picnic lunch and even have an exercise session afterwards. He is free next Saturday afternoon – the 13th, until 6 PM when he holds evening surgery hours for his patients who work during the day. We could pick you up around 1 PM. Is that all right?"

"Sure," Guy replied, as he wrote the appointment in his daybook.

"And then," Luca continued, "I've finally followed through on my promise to help you with your genealogy search. Remember I told you our former parish priest was a cantankerous old man who had no interest in helping genealogists?"

"Yes."

"And I told you the current priest, who is younger and more sympathetic to this issue has been trying to order the parish records, in order to accommodate such searches?"

"Yes."

"Well, I have arranged for you to visit him on Tuesday the 16th, at 2 PM. You remember the Zambri family church I took you to on the Corso? The parish house is behind it. Please bring me any information you find there, and I'll photocopy it on the machine at my shop for myself and the twins."

"Great! What's the priest's name?"

"Father Leonardo. I'll call him this afternoon and confirm the tentative appointment I made for you."

"Thank you."

"Lastly, I must tell you, Guy, that it saddens me you shall be leaving soon and have seen so little of Sicily. Actually, you've only seen Taormina and Messina. That driver you hired to bring you here from the Palermo Airport, when you first arrived, only had one thing in mind – speeding back home to his family. So you really didn't get a tour."

"That's true."

"Now, I know we planned for me to drive you to Palermo on the 30th, so you would be near the airport for your early connecting fight to Rome the next morning. And we planned to spend that night at a hotel there, seeing a bit of Palermo in the process. Well, I am disturbed that you will see so little of Sicily on this trip, if we follow this plan. I know you are busy with your book, but you may never return, and I feel I owe you a decent tour of the land of your ancestors. What I am proposing, is that we leave here early on the morning of Sunday the 28th and drive south to Syracuse. Then west to the fabulous Roman villa at Piazza Armerina – the place with the incredible mosaics. Then on to Agrigento – the Valley of the Temples. And then to Monreale — with its wonderful monastery. We would eventually wind up in Palermo the day before your flight – as we originally planned."

"It sounds *fabulous*, Luca! As an art historian, I would certainly love to do all *that* before leaving."

"Then it is decided. Prepare for us to leave early on Sunday the 28th."

"I will. Perhaps I ought to let the portinari know I'll be vacating early. The Marconis have been nice to me, and I want to be considerate to them. This will allow them a few extra days to clean this apartment before the next tenant arrives."

"I think that would be a nice gesture on your part. My God – look at the time! I must get back to the shop. Anyway, if I don't talk to you before then, Roberto and I will pick you up on Saturday, around 1 PM, for the pictures."

"Yes."

Guy walked Luca to the door, and they kissed and embraced as they had upon Luca's arrival. As Guy closed the door and heard Luca's footsteps descending the stairs to the courtyard, he felt a shiver up his

spine at the thought of seeing all the historic art treasures Luca mentioned, before returning to D.C. And
it didn't hurt to know that he and Luca would be
sharing hotel rooms during his final nights in Sicily!

· FIFTEEN ·

Luca and Roberto seemed to be in a jolly mood when they picked up Guy at the Villa Paradiso on Saturday. After Guy squeezed into the back seat of Luca's little car, next to a large picnic basket upon which lay Luca's camera, Roberto asked — "So, are you ready to shed your clothes and exhibit your *jewels* for the admiration of generations to come?"

Guy turned slightly red and replied, "If you mean am I ready to be photographed for the Brotherhood's archives – yes. I don't know how jewel-like the results will be!"

Luca interjected, "Like *all* Zambri men, you have *nothing* to be ashamed of – below the waist!"

The trio continued to joke and laugh about the day's events in this school-boy fashion as they sped toward Pietro Stanza's farm. When they reached the gate, it was locked – Pietro wasn't home. Roberto jumped out of the car, looked around to see if anyone were watching, and then dislodged a stone in the wall. He removed a key, unlocked and then relocked the gate, returning the key to its hiding place after Luca had driven through. Roberto then jumped back into the car for the short ride to the palaestra building. After he parked, Luca grabbed his camera from the back seat and asked Guy to bring the picnic basket with him. Once they entered the locker room, they set these items down on the bench and Roberto and Luca immediately started to undress. Guy followed their lead and did the same. When they were naked, Luca motioned to Guy to follow him and Roberto into the palaestra, where he opened the armoire that had held the towels the night of Guy's initiation. The cabinet appeared to be stacked with freshly-laundered white towels, but Luca reached down to the bottom shelf and pulled out three items – also solid white in color. He handed one each to Guy and Roberto. As Luca and Roberto put them on, Guy realized they were lightweight bathrobes. He followed suit. After they were all robed, Roberto said, "We need some props." With that, he headed toward the small stage at the end of the room. Shelving, which would not be visible to those sitting in the audience, was at each end of the stage and remained concealed even when the curtains were opened for a performance. Various items were on the shelves, and Guy quickly realized they were similar to props which often appeared in the Baron's photos. Luca pulled down an Arab head-dress from a high shelf, while Roberto gathered up a vase and an animal skin. "I think this will be enough, don't you?" Luca said to Roberto. The latter replied, "Yes, I think so – let's go."

As they exited the building, Guy was directed to bring the picnic basket. Luca carried his camera and the Arab headdress, Roberto the animal skin and the vase. The three robed figures made their way from the palaestra building to the grove, following a narrow path. The grove was small and they soon emerged into a narrow open area, overlooking the sea. Guy immediately recognized it from many of the Baron's photos. A stone wall, which protected one from falling down the cliff and onto the beach, was also tall enough to prevent anyone on the beach from looking up and seeing more than the head and shoulders of persons standing against it. Next to the wall was an ancient stone bench, with some classical carvings on either end. Guy shuddered in excitement as he thought of all the beautiful young ephebes who had posed on *that* bench, over the years. Luca suggested they deposit the items they were carrying on the bench, while they considered how to handle the photography session. As they were doing so, Roberto made a 'knowing' gesture toward Luca, while Guy was distracted by the wonderful view of the sea. Roberto then said, "Perhaps Guy might photograph *us* first, Luca – to get things going?"

Luca immediately recognized Roberto's attempt to put Guy at ease, and he responded, "That sounds like a good idea, doesn't it, Guy?"

Guy smiled, a bit relieved that he wasn't going to immediately plunge into this activity — which both exhilarated him and made him feel self-conscious. "Okay – but I warn you, I'm not a *good* photographer."

"That's okay," Roberto chuckled. "We trust you." As he said these words, he opened his robe, took it off, and hung it on a tree branch – out of the range of the camera. In the early afternoon sunlight, his hirsute body glistened. Even before Guy could instinctively lower his eyes to Roberto's stunning crotch, Luca had shed his robe too, hung it on the same tree branch, and stood beside Roberto. Luca's smooth body was in delightfully sharp contrast to Roberto's, and their awesome fore-skinned dicks almost took Guy's breath away.

Guy started to fumble with Luca's camera, until Luca came over and showed him how it operated. When Guy felt comfortable enough with it, Luca stepped over to the bench and removed the picnic basket and props, so they would be out of camera range. He then said to Roberto, "How about you and I together?"

"Okay," Roberto replied, as he stepped over to the wall and leaned against it. Luca came over and stood beside him. They put their arms around each other's waists, and gazed into each other's eyes. "We're ready," Luca called out to Guy. Guy raised the camera and looked through the viewer. He could see almost fifty years of love in the mutual gaze of these two men, who first embraced in pre-adolescence. He took the photo, silently praying that he had captured this wonderful moment.

Luca and Roberto disengaged and Roberto suggested Guy take a back shot of them, looking out to the sea. Guy remembered a famous von Gloeden shot like this of three ephebes, taken from behind, while standing next to this very wall. Their asses were breath-taking and put to shame any female renditions he had ever seen, in art books, of *The Three Graces*. After Luca and Roberto were in position, Guy took the picture.

"And now, my Cousin, it is your turn," Luca said with a smile. "But first, you must get rid of that robe."

After handing Luca the camera, Guy removed his robe and hung it on a nearby tree branch, as the others had done. Any feelings of discomfort were banished when he saw his comrades surveying his body, from head-to-toe, while Roberto said to Luca, "With that foreskin, he's a Zambri all right!"

Guy chuckled, enjoying how young he felt today. Even on the way here in the car, Luca and Roberto bantered in adolescent double-entendre fashion, making it difficult to believe they were sixty years old. Perhaps, Guy thought, their sense of humor helps them stay so young in appearance and outlook.

"Come here, Guy," Roberto ordered. "I think you'll feel more comfortable doing this for the first time if we take one of you with me, and then one with Luca."

Guy obeyed and came over to Roberto, who had seated himself on the stone bench and had put on the Arab headdress. "Here, sit beside me and lean your head against my chest," Roberto requested. Guy arranged himself as directed. He wasn't sure where to look, though. Just then Luca called out, "Guy, look off in the distance – not at the camera or Roberto. Roberto, you look off in the other direction. I want this to appear as if you are both 'lost' in your thoughts. That's it. Hold still. There – I've got it. Now, let me switch places with Roberto. Here Roberto, take the camera."

Luca walked over to the bench and stopped to think for a moment. Before he could speak, Roberto said, "For the archives, we should have a photo that shows the bond between the Zambri cousins."

"Exactly what I was thinking," Luca replied.

"Okay," Roberto said, with the authority of a film director, "both of you stand straight and proud, staring at each other. Put your arms around each others' necks, but stand far enough apart so that your cocks are not obscured. Good. Now stare at each other like *equals*, not older man-ephebe or father-son."

Luca and Guy assumed the pose to Roberto's satisfaction, and after he took the picture, Luca went over to the picnic basket and removed a bottle of red wine and three glasses. He poured out wine for all of them and passed the glasses around. As they drank, he said, "I think it's time for your solo shots, don't you, Guy?"

"Yes, I'm as ready as I'll ever be!"

At that, Luca directed Roberto to spread the animal skin over the stone bench. After that was done, he directed Guy to sit on the skin – looking casual, but with his legs definitely spread apart, so that his whole "package" showed. Guy recognized this pose as the favored "buffalo shot" in gay porn magazines, and was amused to think that now *he* was to be the admired image for a change, rather than the perpetual admirer.

Luca raised the camera to focus, but put it down, saying in exasperation, "Your balls are being partially obscured by the fur on the skin."

Guy reached down and tried to resolve the problem, but Luca was still dissatisfied. Roberto came forward and offered, "May I? After all, I am a licensed physician."

"Oh yes, gentle physician," Guy chuckled. "Please arrange my package."

Roberto gently lifted Guy's balls while he flattened down the unruly fur on the old animal skin. Then he placed them back in a position which met with Luca's approval.

After that shot was successfully made, Luca suggested Guy stand up and look out toward the sea. The pose looked too static, so Luca asked him to kneel on the stone bench with one knee and lean forward a bit so the crack in his buttocks was slightly open. "I don't want your pink rosebud to show, but I want the 'suggestion' that it is almost in view."

Guy tried to adjust himself to Luca's demands, but the desired pose was still not forthcoming. At this point, Roberto interjected, "May I help? After all, I am a licensed physician." At that, all three men started to giggle uncontrollably. Luca put down the camera and refilled the wine glasses. After a few sips all around, he said, "Are we ready now?"

"Yes," Guy and Roberto responded, in unison.

"Okay," Luca said. "Roberto, go over there and position his ass for my camera. You know what I'm going for." Guy turned back toward the sea, putting one knee on the bench, and patiently waited while Roberto's strong, sure hands adjusted his legs and buttocks to Luca's satisfaction. It crossed Guy's mind that he had gradually come to view his Beloved Cousin, Luca, as a perfectionist, and somewhat of a "control freak". But, he was glad Luca was of such a temperament, because the archivist of a secret organization such as the Brotherhood needed to be – if records were to survive in good order.

Roberto stepped back, Guy held the pose, and didn't relax until Luca shouted, "Okay – I've got it."

They looked around, trying to decide on the next shot, and when Guy spotted the vase they had brought from the palaestra, he suggested a pose. "How about this? It will be a scene of offering to the pagan gods, by a proud, naked man who faces them directly." With that, Guy picked up the vase, which had a classical shape, and held it high above his head, like an offering. He spread his legs, straightened his back, and looked up beyond the raised vase, toward the bright heavens.

"Perfect!" Luca shouted.

"Yes," Roberto agreed.

Luca took the shot, from *two* angles, because he loved it so. "Wonderful, wonderful. But you know, friends, I'm hungry now. Let's eat. I think we have enough photos to document Guy's membership in the Brotherhood."

The others agreed, and Roberto quickly spread a tablecloth, taken from the picnic basket, along the ground. While Luca put away his camera, Guy laid out the cheese, bread, olives and grapes he found in the basket. Roberto poured more wine, and they hungrily ate in near-silence, until Guy grabbed the large bunch of grapes from the tablecloth and placed it in front of his crotch. "I am Bacchus, God of Wine. Come taste my sweet offerings." With that, he walked over to where Luca was sitting and shoved his crotch in Luca's face. Luca chuckled and nibbled at several of the grapes. Then, Guy turned to Roberto, who nibbled several more, until Guy's cockhead was exposed. As Guy started to turn away to go back to where he had been sitting, he felt Roberto's lips momentarily graze his foreskin. He was *thrilled*.

When the meal was over, Luca suggested they adjourn to the palaestra to get some exercise. He reminded Roberto that the latter had office hours at his surgery on Saturday nights for his working patients, so they would have to head back to Taormina around 5 PM. It was already 2:30 PM, so they retrieved the robes from their resting places in the trees, put them back on, and gathered up the items they had brought to the grove. Once back in the locker room they undressed again and left the robes on the bench for Pietro to launder later. After they replaced the props on the shelves near the stage, Roberto asked

Guy, "Are you familiar with Greco-Roman wrestling?"

Luca looked in Guy's direction. "Remember I told you it is a favorite of Roberto's?"

"Yes, I remember. And no, I don't know anything about it, except for references in literature and art."

"Well," Roberto explained, "all the rules are the same as in free-style wrestling – except for two: no holds are allowed *below* the waist, and the legs can't be used to take down one's opponent. Did you ever do any wrestling in the past?"

"A little, in high school gym class – the free-style kind."

"Well, this was added to the modern Olympics in 1906, and I love it for many reasons – but especially because it is a pure reincarnation of sport among the ancients."

"And don't you regret that you can't grab hold of anything *beneath* your opponent's waist?" Guy said, with a lecherous chuckle.

Roberto rolled his eyes and looked toward Luca. "Your cousin is a satyr at heart, I think." And then to Guy, "There is plenty of time for *that* after the match is over. Now, do you want to try it?"

"Perhaps you and Luca should go first?"

"Oh no!" Luca exclaimed. "I've had years of being pinned to the mat by this 'man-bull'. It's *your* turn!" Then he added, "I had hoped some of the other Brothers would be here today, working out, but I guess we're going to be all alone. I think I'll go over to the weights and work with them."

"So, it's settled?" Roberto asked.

"Yes," Guy replied. "What do I do?"

"Come with me to the mats," Roberto directed. Guy joined him on one of the mats and Roberto showed him how to get into the starting position. After a brief review of holds and rules – requested by Guy, since he hadn't wrestled since high school, they began to tussle. No matter what Guy did, time and again Roberto took him down and quickly pinned his shoulders to the mat. Even with Roberto's instructions on how to avoid his traps, Guy still could not savor a single victory. After a time, he was exhausted, and just lay on the mat, begging for a cessation of the exercise.

Roberto leaned over Guy, who was flat on his back from the last pinning, and said, "So, you have had enough of this?"

"Yes. It was interesting *and* fun, but I have had enough, Roberto."

Roberto bent down and took Guy in his arms. His pelted chest almost smothered Guy as he pressed it to the latter's face. The combined scent of sweat and man-musk from their bodies was overwhelming. "So, would you like to try *another* sport? One at which you seemed very adept during your initiation ceremony?"

Guy glanced nervously over at Luca, who was grunting loudly under the stress of the weights he hoisted. He was sure Roberto was referring to the "69" he and Luca had performed while Roberto screwed the brains out of the man with the damaged foot that night. "I would love to do that with you, Roberto. You have been so kind to me, and did so much to bring me into the Brotherhood on such short notice, before I leave here. But, I love my Cousin, Luca, and would not want to disrespect him."

"I understand. But has Luca not told you he and I have been lovers since we were lads?"

"Yes. But wouldn't that make it even *more* hurtful for him to see us making love here today?"

"Not at all. In the Brotherhood we harbor no jealousy. Our relations with each other are like what you Americans call an 'open marriage'. The Brothers joyfully partake of the pleasure of each others' bodies – as long as it is consensual."

"So, you are saying Luca would consent?"

At this, Roberto turned away from Guy and looked in Luca's direction. "Luca," he called across the room. "Could you come here for a minute?"

Luca looked up, put down the weights, and walked over to the mat upon which his companions lay. Roberto looked up at him and said, "I have invited your Cousin to make love – here and now. But he is reluctant because he fears that to do so would show you disrespect."

Luca smiled down at Guy, momentarily. Then he knelt beside the mat, and bent over – taking Guy's head in both his hands. He kissed Guy on the forehead and repeated the gesture with Roberto. Without saying a word, he rose and returned to his weights.

Roberto turned and cradled Guy in his arms again. "Okay, now?"

"I guess so. But, I'm not exactly sure what just happened here."

"Let me tell you a story," Roberto began. "Several years ago, Luca and I came out here for a session of exercise and love on a Sunday afternoon. Luca's wife was spending the weekend in Naxos with her family. As I recall, it was the anniversary of her father's death and they were having special masses said for him. The twins were old enough to be left to their own devices, so they stayed home. Shortly after we arrived at the palaestra, one of the Brothers injured his hand while exercising on some of this equipment. I had no choice but to take him to my surgery, as he needed an x-ray and was bleeding. Luca dropped the patient and myself off and decided to call it a day – returning home earlier than expected. Apparently, the twins didn't hear him climb the stairs and enter the apartment. But he could hear low voices coming from their room. Have you ever seen it?"

Guy nodded.

"Then you know it's very small, with a pair of narrow beds pushed against opposite walls, and just enough space between them for one person to walk at a time. Anyway, as he passed their bedroom door, he casually glanced in – the door was ajar. Dario was in Mario's bed and they were making love. As he later told the story to me, Luca said he was momentarily transfixed by their adolescent love – a love so universal among boys that he found himself recalling the many times he and I stole away to be in each others' arms at that age. Anyway, before he could quietly leave the doorway and go back downstairs – returning with a commotion which would have given the twins plenty of time to uncouple, Mario spotted him and shouted "Papa!" Dario spun around and after seeing Luca, dove back into his own bed. Both boys then covered their faces with their bedspreads. Without saying a word, Luca walked into the narrow space between the beds, leaned down and pulled off Dario's bedspread with his left hand and Mario's with his right. The boys tried to cover their faces with their hands now, and cowered in fear. Then, Luca leaned over, took Dario's head in both hands, and kissed him on the forehead. He did the same to Mario, turned around, left the room and closed the door behind him. He called them to dinner several hours later, and nothing more was said of the matter – even to this day. So why am I telling you this? What does it mean?"

"I guess it means he was giving them his *blessing* – with the silent kiss."

"Yes. By that simple action, he was telling them that what they were doing was all right with him, natural, normal and healthy. And, I might add, he just told us the same thing – did he not?"

Guy chuckled. "Yes – I guess he did."

"One other thing," Roberto added. "Not long after that, I came home from my surgery unexpectedly – my nurse suddenly took ill and had to go home, so I closed the office and left a note on the door on how I could be reached for emergencies. It must have been around Christmas, because my wife and her best girlfriend were in Messina, holiday shopping for a few days. Anyway, Fredo apparently didn't hear me come in, and as I passed his room and glanced in, I found him sprawled naked on his bed, masturbating. As soon as he saw me, he ducked beneath the covers, as had Luca's twins on the occasion I just described. Now, Fredo and I had talked about sex over the years, but in a very *clinical* fashion. He's wanted to be a physician since he was quite young, so I've made my medical texts available to him and he's often asked questions about what he's read in them or seen in the illustrations. When he was about thirteen, I realized we had never talked about sex in a *personal* way, so I gave him a book written especially for adolescent boys and invited him to discuss anything in it that he wanted. He read it, but never asked me any questions. The day I caught him masturbating, I was momentarily uncertain what to do, but then I remembered Luca's episode with the twins. So, I just went over to his bed, pulled back the covers, took his head in both my hands, kissed him on the forehead, turned, and left the room – closing the door behind me, without saying a word."

"And in that silent action, you spoke volumes – volumes that overcame the dangerous nonsense fathers have told their sons for generations about one of the most normal acts a man can perform."

"Yes. I shared this episode with Luca, and together we were proud to know our sons were growing into men. Fredo and the twins are best friends – the three of them are nearly inseparable. Luca and I assume they engage in circle jerks and the like – which is fine with us. The local school's gymnasium is open on Saturdays for use by students and their parents, so Luca and I try to join the boys at least twice a month for exercise sessions there. It is a great bonding experience for fathers and sons to help each other build strong bodies, side by side. And the communal showers afterwards seal that bond even more. The boys would like us to join them *every* Saturday, but Luca and the twins can't go unless Theresa will watch the shop, and she insists on going to her sister's in Naxos several weekends a month. Then too, Luca and I need to get away to come here, because it is a refuge for our lovemaking, as well as for keeping our bodies strong. Sometimes, we just can't get to the palaestra for weeks at a time, so we steal moments at my surgery after the staff and patients have all left for the day."

"How do you get away from the boys to come here — without them, or your wives, getting suspicious?"

"We both belong to a variety of local organizations – commercial, civic, fraternal, religious. It's easy to make up an excuse to go work on some organizational project or other. It will be a blessing, in more ways than one, if Fredo and the twins are receptive to the Brotherhood when they are approached individually, after they come of age in about four years. Then, there will be no more need for lies between us. But, there's no guarantee they will want to join."

"Why not?"

"Let's save that discussion for another day. I have office hours tonight and Luca has given his blessing. Shall we make love?"

Guy snuggled up to Roberto's neck, and with a light kiss, said, "Yes."

Roberto kissed him back, hard and deep, on the mouth. Then he rose, walked over to the supply armoire, took out condoms, and returned to the mat. Roberto threw one down to Guy, who put it on promptly, while he stood over him, in full erection, dressing his own cock. When he lay down, Roberto assumed the sixty-nine position and immediately began to hungrily devour Guy. Guy responded in kind. Their ejaculatory moans of delight, minutes later, were heard by Luca across the room. Luca smiled at the joy between these two men, both of whom he loved.

As was his custom, Guy quickly started to fall asleep after sex. Just before he lost consciousness, his tongue found one of Roberto's hard nipples, buried in the forest of his chest hair. He licked it and sucked on it as long as he could.

It was Luca's body, pressing against his back, that woke Guy later. He found himself squeezed between Luca and Roberto, like the sandwich filling between two slices of bread. "Ah, my Cousin, you are awake," Luca said. "Will you spread your thighs a bit so I may take my pleasure?"

Guy smiled and spread his thighs a couple of inches. Luca had procured a bottle of lubricant from the armoire and covered his bare cock with it. Then, minus a condom, he slipped his hard dick between Guy's thighs. Guy tightened them as Luca thrust in and out. Roberto whispered in Guy's ear, "This is the interfemoral – intercrural sex I told you about. It was a favorite of the ancients. Luca uses no condom, since he has not entered you."

"It is an honor for me to give pleasure to my Cousin," Guy responded, as he absorbed every pounding thrust from behind.

After Luca came, splattering his love-milk all over the mat and between Guy's legs, he rolled off Guy and wiped up the mess with a small hand-towel. The three of them lay there hugging and kissing for awhile, before Luca glanced at his wristwatch and said, "We must shower and get Roberto to his surgery."

The three of them picked up the debris that accumulated from their lovemaking and took it to the trash can which stood between the two armoires. They then removed clean bath towels from the linen armoire and went to the shower room. The three of them stood under a single showerhead, soaping each other down, in between caresses, hugs and kisses. Despite their recent ejaculations, all three remained hard. After they had rinsed off and Luca was about to reach up and shut off the shower faucet, Guy dropped to his knees and began to massage Luca's left leg and thigh. Then he did the same to the right one. He shifted a bit and provided the same service to Roberto. Both men had hard-muscled legs and thighs, and the tactile pleasure Guy received from the massages he gave almost made him cum again. Finally, he threw his arms around all four of their legs, hugged them dearly, and bent down and kissed each of their water-soaked feet. As he looked up into their beautiful faces and started to rise, Luca grabbed him under one arm, and Roberto under the other. They simultaneously pulled him up into their waiting arms, where they kissed passionately under the steady stream of water.

Later, in the locker room, they lovingly toweled each other off. After they dressed, they piled the dirty towels and robes on one end of the bench, for Pietro to gather up for laundering. Then, Luca took up his camera, and Roberto took up the picnic basket – while Guy went to shut off all the lights in the building. As they passed the small, slotted wooden box near the door, they each deposited lira for Pietro.

On the way back into town, Guy was in a state of exhaustion. *What a day*, he thought. He sat mute while Luca and Roberto made small-talk in the front seat. At the surgery, Guy gave Roberto a quick hug and kiss as the latter got out of the car, waved goodbye and walked to his door – carrying the picnic basket.

A few minutes later, Luca deposited Guy in front of the Villa Paradiso, promising to develop the film in his camera promptly. As he pulled away from the curb, he shouted to Guy, "Remember – Tuesday at 2 PM for genealogy with Father Leonardo!"

· SIXTEEN ·

As Guy turned the corner to enter the Corso for his 2 PM appointment to do genealogy research on the Zambri family at the family's longtime parish church, he glanced at his wristwatch and noted he was going to be early. Deciding it would not be politic to prematurely disturb the parish priest with whom Luca had arranged this appointment, Guy decided to pass some time visiting Luca in his shop. However, as he approached Luca's place, he saw a family of five tourists enter. He guessed they were Americans, in view of their stereotypically gaudy tourist garb, and decided to leave Luca alone while he dealt with them.

Proceeding down the street, he remembered that he still hadn't bought Chad a gift for watching his apartment and mail. So, he spent some time window-shopping in the hope that he would *finally* complete that task, as his days in Sicily were quickly drawing to a close. Soon, he found himself staring in the window of a jewelry store. As he gazed at the expensive rings and wristwatches in the window – none of which were within his price range, he was aware that someone from inside the store had come out and was standing in the open doorway. He instinctively glanced up as the gentleman in the doorway said, "Good afternoon, Sir."

Guy responded, "Good afternoon," and quickly turned his gaze back toward the contents of the window. He really resented when merchants rushed out of their shops to engage potential customers in conversation as the latter looked at the display merchandise – in the hopes the potential customer could be lured inside the store to close a sale.

As Guy stood there, annoyed by this "intrusion", he heard the man say "Beautiful Taormina afternoon, isn't it?" Guy looked in his direction again and replied, "Yes," – however this time he noticed the man himself – about mid-twenties and wearing a beautiful Italian suit with a silk shirt. The shirt was open at the neck – no tie in this Sicilian heat. After Guy returned his gaze to the window and was looking at the more moderately-priced gold and silver money clips on display, he had the vague feeling this gentleman looked familiar. He took a step backward to read the words painted on the shop's window: *R. Massi and Son, Jewelers.*

R. Massi, Guy thought. Yes – the Brother who Luca told him had designed the medallion for the Brotherhood! This must be his shop. When Guy looked up again at the figure standing in the doorway, the latter was smiling broadly at him. Guy now recognized him as the ephebic "Ganymede" who posed with Roberto during the tableaux vivants at his initiation ceremony. Now, in his mind's eye, Guy saw him not in his business finery, but naked, shaved, smooth, hung and beautiful – as on that night. The man – obviously Raphael Massi's son, casually reached into the open neck of his shirt, and after glancing around to see if anyone were watching, lifted out several inches of thin gold chain from around his neck. Guy smiled, reached under the collar of his open-necked shirt and did the same. Guy and Massi's son then nodded and smiled again at each other — in secret, silent recognition of their bond, before Guy hurried away, down the street, toward the parish house.

By the time he reached the front door of the priest's residence – behind the church as Luca had said, he was trying to deflate the raging hard-on that had resulted from his encounter with his beautiful Brother – Massi the Younger. Within seconds of ringing the bell, the door opened to reveal a tiny, elderly Sicilian woman, completely covered in black widow's garb from head to toe. On her feet were a pair of old, scruffy – but undoubtedly comfortable, slippers. After Guy introduced himself, she said, "Ah yes. I am Anna, the parish housekeeper. Father Leonardo is expecting you. Come with me, Sir."

Guy followed her down a short hallway, amused at the way she shuffled her feet along the floor, rather than pick them up, one foot at a time. When they reached a set of double doors, she ushered him into a room containing a large desk, with a chair behind it – and two chairs, obviously for visitors, in front of it. There were several large bookcases in the room, and several religious pictures on the walls – the Madonna, the Sacred Heart, and assorted saints. Off to one side of the room was an alcove, from which Guy heard a man shout, "Have Mr. Zambri take a seat, Anna. I'll be right with him." At that, Anna directed Guy to one of the chairs in front of the desk, turned, left the room, and closed the double doors behind her.

Guy sat patiently for a few minutes, examining the contents of the room, from where he sat – and listening to the sound of rustling papers that emanated from the alcove. Finally, he saw a cassock-draped figure emerging from the alcove and coming toward him. Guy rose to accept the outstretched hand of the priest, whom he now faced directly. They were about the same height, and the first thing Guy noted was Father Leonardo's incredible green eyes. Then he noticed his ginger-colored/reddish brown hair. *My God,* Guy thought – *it's one of the Gemini twins from my initiation!*

Guy's body went numb as the priest gave him a hearty handshake, and bade him to sit down again. Guy was too befuddled to comprehend Father Leonardo's initial conversational banter, but assuming the priest was making perfunctory social comments, he kept nodding his head in agreement. He struggled to regain his composure, and did so just as Father Leonardo was saying, "So, your Cousin, Luca, tells me you came to Taormina to do genealogical research on the Zambris."

"Yes – partly, that is. I'm an art historian and I'm also writing a book. I'm actually on sabbatical leave from my university to work on the book."

"I see. Well, I'm sure Luca has told you that the parish records I inherited were in a state of disarray for years. My predecessor was a dear old man, but he had absolutely *no* interest in dealing with hordes of foreign tourists scouring for their ancestors, through the parish's records. Shortly after I arrived about three years ago, it occurred to me that any investment I made in accommodating researchers might help the parish in the long run — especially if visitors left a donation, for our services. Am I being too crass, Mr. Zambri?"

"Not at all," Guy laughed. "I know you can't pay the electric bill and other parish expenses through prayer alone!"

"Exactly. Anyway, there was no way that I could possibly straighten out the old records on my own – I just had too many other responsibilities. So, I decided to tap into the energy of the young. We have several teenagers in the parish who are already very proficient with computers, so I formed a club for them. Their first task was to create a program for monitoring the parish's financial records – then membership lists and other high-priority data. About a year ago, we were finally ready to deal with genealogy. Someone, earlier in the century, had cleaned up the records back to about 1850. I don't know who. I assume an energetic, young priest, new to the parish, with a fascination for history. Anyway, the youngsters in my club have taken us back to about 1800. Here, let me show you."

With that, Father Leonardo ushered Guy into the adjoining alcove. The alcove was almost completely filled with an old long rectangular table that served as a desk. On top of it sat a computer, with a printer on one side and a copier on the other. There was a stack of shiny leather-bound volumes at the end of the table, and computer paper and other office supplies on nearby shelving. An office chair sat directly in front of the computer. Pointing to the books, Father Leonardo said, "These are the records we sent to Rome for conservation. They used special processes there to treat the pages for insect damage, mildew, damage to the paper and the ink, and so forth. Then, the leather bindings were cleaned and refurbished. After that, the students went through them and entered the data into the computer. We only had enough money to send these volumes for conservation, but we have many more which we hope to also send one day."

"I see," Guy said, impressed with the priest's effort.

Father Leonardo then picked up a manual and said to Guy, "Look at this and tell me if you understand it, as it tells one how to access the genealogical files." Guy sat down in the chair which was positioned in front of the computer and correctly followed the commands which gave him access to the parish records on births, baptisms, marriages and deaths – back to 1800.

"Wonderful!" Father Leonardo replied. "You obviously read Italian as well as you speak it. Where did you learn?"

Guy blushed a bit at the complement, then said, "Thank you. No one is more surprised than I over how little trouble I've had communicating since I arrived here. My grandfather – who was born in Taormina and raised me, taught me to speak Italian. Actually, the Taorminian/Sicilian dialect he knew – not the upper-class Tuscan dialect taught in school."

"Ah yes," Father Leonardo responded, with a broad smile, as he stared intently at Guy while the latter continued: "Then, I took several years of Italian in college. The college courses have helped me to *read* Italian more than to *speak* it."

"I see. Well, you seem to be quite proficient."

"It helps that so many of the local merchants speak English – at least partially."

Father Leonardo smiled again, and responded, "The Taorminian merchants learned decades ago that they had better learn English and German if they wanted to fully exploit the tourist possibilities around here. For years, British and German tourists kept the local economy going. And of course now, we have the Americans – in droves."

"Yes, you do."

"Anyway," Father Leonardo continued, "I shall leave you to your task. I have a sermon to work on for next Sunday. I'll be at my desk nearby, in case you have any questions."

"Thank you, Father," Guy said, as he turned toward the computer and began to enter the Zambri family name, and the names of Angelo, Rocco and Amadeo – for starters. As Guy worked, he was aware of Father Leonardo taking a phone call or two at his desk, or moving papers or books around, but he remained fully concentrated on the task at hand. After about an hour and a half, he had located all the Zambris he could find, back to 1800. Father Leonardo's student club had done an admirable job of setting up a clear, simple program for this kind of research. As he worked, he printed out a copy of the Zambri information he found, intending to drop by Luca's shop afterward so he could make copies for him and his sons. After shutting off the computer and gathering up his materials, he remembered it would be appropriate to leave a donation. He searched through his wallet and was happy to find several large bills. He counted out the equivalent of fifty U.S. dollars, put them in one of the small white envelopes he found on a nearby shelf, sealed it, and addressed it to the computer club. As he emerged from the alcove, he said to Father Leonardo, "Well, I believe I have exhausted your records on the Zambris – at least back to 1800."

"Wonderful," Father Leonardo responded. "Perhaps one day we will have more of them in order and you can return."

"Would that I could," Guy remarked. "I'd love to come back to Taormina one day, but who knows what the future holds?" Then, turning morose, he added, "Those people who went to work on 9/11 at the World Trade Center...." His voice trailed off at this point.

"I know," Father Leonardo said, in his best pastoral counseling voice, "What a horrible tragedy. We all feel for your countrymen."

"Thank you," Guy said quietly. Then, with raised spirits he said – as he handed the white envelope with the lira to the priest, "A little something for the continued operation of your computer club."

"Why thank you. The students will be thrilled. And now, before you go, I hope you will take tea with me?"

"Oh, Father, I wouldn't want to inconvenience you."

"Not at all. It has been planned ever since your cousin made this appointment for you. Anna is just waiting for me to summon her by pressing this buzzer on my desk. See – watch how quickly she will appear. Please sit in one of these chairs near my desk."

Within a few minutes, Anna opened the double doors, retrieved a large tray she had temporarily placed on a chest in the hall, and laid it on Father Leonardo's desk.

Both Father Leonardo and Guy expressed admiration for her culinary artistry – assorted finger sandwiches and Sicilian pastry, as she blushed and backed out of the room, closing the doors behind her.

Father Leonardo came over to the front of the desk, poured tea for both himself and Guy, filled a plate with food, and bade Guy to do the same. After the priest was settled again in his chair behind the desk and was enjoying his food, he and Guy made small-talk for awhile.

When they had both eaten their fill, and were draining their second cup of tea, Father Leonardo suddenly said to Guy, "Since you are an art historian, you could do me a great service before you leave by interpreting an unusual print I have."

Guy was a bit surprised by the request, as he automatically glanced around the room at the religious art hanging on the walls of the priest's study.

"Oh, not anything like *those*," Father Leonardo said, with a laugh. At that, he picked up a set of keys that had been lying on his desk since Guy's arrival and unlocked one of his desk drawers. He pulled out a brown folder which had a large elastic band around it, and removed a sheet of paper. As he handed it to Guy he said, "Here, what do you make of this?"

Guy took the print and stared at it momentarily. Then he burst into a broad grin.

"I see you recognize it," Father Leonardo said.

"Yes, I do. It's by a Frenchman named Jean Delville. It's owned by the French government and is in the Musee D'Orsay in Paris. I first saw it in a volume they published. Since that time, I've seen it reproduced in several other books."

"Can you explain it? I mean, I see a figure who looks very like Christ the Nazarene, sitting under a tree. There are twelve men around him – six on either side. But they hardly look like the twelve apostles!"

"Well," Guy began, "it's called *The School of Plato*. Actually, some translate the French title as *Plato's Academy*."

"So, the central figure is Plato, teaching a philosophy lesson?"

"Yes and no. It can be read as Plato teaching a class. However, the central figure's iconography is more Christ-like than that we associate with Plato."

"But the other figures hardly look like the apostles. They are mostly nude, languid, and quite – effeminate."

"And so we have the conundrum," Guy replied. "The most-widely accepted interpretation of this painting is that Delville has deliberately presented an ambiguous image that can be read as the pagan Plato teaching philosophy to his students under a tree – or as Christ instructing his disciples."

"To what purpose?" Father Leonardo asked.

"To show the influence of the pagan world on the Christian world. An influence that continues to this day – in many of our religious holidays, for instance, which were originally pagan festivals expropriated by the early Church to woo converts. And, of course, in much of Christian art. That painting of the Madonna on your wall, for instance."

Father Leonardo turned and looked at the Madonna's portrait hanging on the wall behind his desk. "For instance?"

"Well," Guy continued – after nervously clearing his throat, "many see Mary as the *re-presentation* of many previous pagan goddesses."

Father Leonardo reached over and took back the print from Guy. He looked at it briefly, and then put it back in the folder, which he re-locked in the desk drawer. He then looked up at Guy, and with a sheepish grin said – in a confessional tone of voice, "I had come to the same conclusion about it some time ago, but I was interested in hearing your analysis, for several reasons."

"Several reasons?"

"Yes. First – because I respect your professional opinion as an art historian."

"And the other reasons?"

"Actually, only one. I was hoping that by analyzing this work of art you would find the answer to the question you've been asking yourself since I shook your hand in greeting earlier in the afternoon."

"The question?" Guy asked, shifting nervously in his chair.

At that point, Father Leonardo rose from his chair and walked over to the study's double doors. He locked them and returned to stand in front of the desk, looking directly down at Guy. He sat on the edge of the desk and started to unbutton the top buttons of his floor-length cassock. Pointing to the Roman collar around his neck he said, "You've been wondering how I can reconcile *this*, with *another* symbol." He then reached down, below his collar, and pulled his Brotherhood medallion into full view.

As Guy stared up at the juxtaposed image of the Roman collar and the Brotherhood's medallion dangling beneath it, Father Leonardo said, "I can juggle *both* these worlds. I have to. They are intrinsically intertwined. They have always been, and they will always be." Then, he slowly began to unbutton his cassock, from the top on down. By the time his red-brown chest hairs were exposed, Guy was already hard. When the priest finished undoing the lowest buttons, which required bending forward, he raised his head and threw open his holy garment. He was in full erection. Guy gasped audibly. Father Leonardo smiled and reached into one of the cassock's pockets, extracting a condom. He dressed himself with it and pulled Guy's head toward his throbbing cock. All this time, Guy's gaze was locked into that of the priest's gem-like green eyes. Guy felt hypnotized by their unusual beauty.

He couldn't take his own eyes off them. Soon, he felt the priest's hard member against his cheek, looked down, and prepared to receive the offering made to him. With his eyes closed, Guy could still see those green gems as he concentrated on giving his Brother pleasure. Father Leonardo's moans were so intense and audible when he came, that Guy started to pull away – but the priest's hands kept his head firmly in place until he was fully satisfied. Slowly, Father Leonardo got up off the desk. He reached down to Guy, pulled him up, and now positioned *him* on the edge of the desk. Guy leaned back and knocked over something on the desktop, with his left hand. He thought it was something from the tea service, but when he looked back he realized Father Leonardo had previously shifted the tray off to one side of his large desk. Guy instinctively picked up the displaced object. It was a framed photo which had faced away from him all afternoon. As he placed the framed photo upright, he glanced at it. It depicted two men with Roman collars – one was Father Leonardo and the other was the man who had been his Gemini twin at Guy's initiation. Father Leonardo, upon observing this, interjected, "My brother. He has a parish over in Naxos."

Guy laughed aloud at the thought that two Catholic priests had posed as the Gemini during his initiation ceremony — and in his joy, quickly opened his shirt, while Father Leonardo eagerly unzipped and lowered his trousers. The priest reached into his cassock pocket again and pulled out another condom, which he placed on Guy's throbbing cock. He then proceeded to devour him, until Guy shuddered and moaned in ecstasy several minutes later.

Afterwards, they cleaned themselves up and Father Leonardo collected the used condoms and their wrappings in a plain envelope he retrieved from the alcove – obviously to dispose of later, out of sight of Anna. As he walked Guy to the double doors he said, "I hope you have found everything you came for today. I hope your stay in Taormina has been delightful. And I hope you have a safe trip home to your troubled nation." At that, he took Guy in his arms and stared him straight in the eyes. Guy's knees started to buckle at such a close view of those green orbs. Father Leonardo caught him before he could fall, held him tight, and then kissed him hard and deep on the mouth. Gaining his composure, Guy reciprocated. Father Leonardo then reached into Guy's shirt and pulled out his medallion – which he kissed. Guy then reached under the priest's Roman collar, retrieved his medallion, and kissed it in return.

As they emerged from the study, Anna came running down the hall to fulfill her duty of showing Guy to the front door. At the door, Guy thanked her profusely for the tea and then turned to Father Leonardo and said, "Your kindness today will be with me forever, Father."

His last image was of Anna standing proudly in the doorway, enjoying the success of her tea-time offerings, and of Father Leonardo beside her, smiling in great satisfaction at having been *one*, if only for a brief period of time, with his new Brother.

As Guy made his way slowly down the Corso to Luca's shop, where he would make copies – for Luca and the twins, of the genealogical information he had located, he wondered how much he should tell his cousin about the afternoon's events.

• SEVENTEEN •

Guy poured himself a drink of cold water from the pitcher in the refrigerator, and sat down in front of the television. He hadn't turned it on much in recent days. The "War on Terror" was raging in Afghanistan, and 9/11 rubble was still being cleared away at the WTC and the Pentagon. These events dominated the news day and night and served only to depress him. Actually, he'd been very busy in recent days – making a final stab at collecting genealogical information, and completing another chapter of his book. And now he was packing for his return home, and completing social engagements. It was Wednesday the 24th and he had a dinner invitation tonight – an unexpected one at that. And on Friday night, he was invited to Dr. Rossi's house for a "farewell" dinner, before he and Luca left on their tour of Sicily. He was delighted that Luca and his family were also invited to Roberto's dinner party.

Tonight's invitation resulted from Guy's having told the Marconis he would be vacating the apartment early on the morning of the 28th – even though his lease ran through the 31st. Stefano and Irini had been very gracious to him the past few months and he felt they would appreciate knowing they had a few extra days to clean the condo before the next tenant arrived. Upon hearing this, Stefano told Guy that all matters related to the lease had to be discussed directly with the leasing agent – Tonio Valli. Guy had dealt with Valli over the internet when he set up the lease, and therefore had his local business address and phone number in case he had any problems that the Marconis couldn't handle. However, he'd not had any reason to contact him during his stay – until this issue arose. Therefore, a few days earlier, he had called Tonio Valli's office.

"May I please speak with Mr. Valli?"

"Speaking."

"Yes. My name is Guy Zambri – I've been renting a condo at the Villa Paradiso since September 1st. I'm vacating it a few days early and when I told the Marconis, they said I needed to talk to you."

"I see. Are you asking for a refund for those days?"

"Oh, no. Not at all. The Marconis have been very helpful during my stay and I just thought they'd appreciate knowing they had several extra days to clean it before the next tenant arrives. That's why I told them. But Stefano said all issues related to the lease have to be handled by you."

"Yes. That's true. Well, I see no problem here. The morning you leave, just give them the key. There'll be a delay of several weeks before I can mail back your security deposit because I have to wait for the telephone company to send your final bill and deduct it from your deposit – along with any damages to the unit."

"Of course. Although I doubt you'll find any damage."

"I'm sure I won't. The Marconis have spoken very highly of you, too. You've been no problem during your stay. Believe it or not, they are sometimes awakened at 3 AM by tenants looking for an aspirin."

"You've got to be kidding!"

"No, I'm not. I could tell you stories about property management, Mr. Zambri! But then, that's not why you called. What day and time are you leaving?"

"About 7:30 AM on Sunday the 28th."

"Humm.....the Marconis will probably have left for early Mass by then. I'll tell you what – put the key in an envelope, write your name on it and slip it through the mail slot on their door if they aren't there. Also, at the risk of sounding presumptuous, if you had planned to leave them a gratuity, you could put it in the same envelope."

By now, Guy was well aware of the importance of tipping the locals who depended on tourists for their livelihood. "Of course. That's a good idea. Thank you. I guess that covers everything. I've enjoyed the Villa Paradiso immensely and will recommend it to my friends."

"I'd appreciate that. Before you ring off, I'd like to invite you to dinner if I may. We rarely get tenants as cooperative and trouble-free as you have been. It would be a small token of *my* appreciation."

"That's very kind of you. I have two problems, however. In these final days I'm on a very tight schedule, and secondly – I don't have a car here, so that limits my mobility."

"Let's take your problems one-by-one. Do you have an opening on Wednesday evening, the 24th?"

"Let me look at my appointment book – its right here. Yes – I do."

"Fine – how about 7PM?"

"That sounds good. And where will I meet you? Is it within walking distance of Villa Paradiso?"

"Yes it is. Here are the directions: Go to your front door and walk down the stairs to the courtyard. Cross the courtyard and go to the staircase near the Marconis apartment. Climb those stairs and knock on the door that's at the top of the stairs."

"You mean *you* live at Villa Paradiso?"

"Yes, I do – upstairs, like yourself, but in the opposite wing."

"I'll be darned! It's strange that we haven't met these past two months."

"I've caught glimpses of you walking in and out of your place or getting into your cousin's car a couple times, but I work such irregular hours, that I'm gone much of the time. I not only manage multiple rental properties but I also sell real estate and am called upon to show property at all hours of the day and night."

"I see. Well, what a surprise. Okay, then – I'll see you Wednesday around 7 PM."

"Till then. Arrivederci!"

Even as Guy recalled this conversation several days later, just before leaving to cross the courtyard and meet Tonio Valli, he still found it ironic that he and the unseen Mr. Valli could have been in such close proximity for nearly two months without his knowing it. At seven, he turned off the TV and the living room lights, and headed over to Valli's apartment. Within seconds of his knocking on the door, it was opened. A short, trim man with brown hair and a thin mustache greeted him. As was his habit, Guy stared into the stranger's eyes first – long believing that the eyes are not only the "mirror of the soul", but often an individual's most attractive feature. Tonio Valli's eyes were the same dull-brown color as his hair and mustache, but his infectious smile made Guy feel comfortable immediately. While they briefly stood in the tiled entrance hallway, Guy said, "Funny we should *finally* meet – after two months of being neighbors!"

Tonio Valli looked Guy directly in the eyes and said, "Actually, we have met before – although it was rather brief."

"We have?" Guy replied, as he followed Valli down the long hallway. As he walked behind his host, he happened to glance down at Valli's feet and noticed one shoe was definitely built up with an extra-thick sole and heel, so Valli could stand straight. Somewhere in his memory bank this rang a bell and then he made the connection, just as Valli turned and said, "We met in the reception line at the Palaestra several weeks ago."

"Of course!" Guy replied, remembering Valli as the man Roberto took doggie-style on a nearby mat, while he and Luca celebrated the Revels. Before Guy could add anything else to cover his embarrassment at not having recognized one of the Brothers who was in the crowd at his initiation, he found himself ushered into a large room – obviously a combination living-dining room. Expensive-looking antiques, heavy furniture and artwork abounded. An ornate carved fireplace was in the middle of one of the long walls of this rectangular-shaped room, and the opposite long wall was pierced by four pairs of French doors – all of which faced the sea and opened onto a huge tiled terrace.

"My God," Guy exclaimed, "this is magnificent!"

"Thank you," Valli replied, smiling with pride. "This was my parents' condo. I – my sister and I — inherited it after their deaths. She and her family live in Messina, but I keep her old bedroom intact for her use, and my old bedroom for her daughters, as they visit often. Later, I'll show you around. For now, why don't we sit on the terrace and have some appetizers?"

"I'd *love* to see the view from there, Mr. Valli!"

"*Tonio* – please. I am known far and wide in this part of Sicily as *Tonio*."

"*Tonio* it is. And please call me *Guy*."

"Thank you, Guy. Here, come out to the terrace."

The terrace was as long as the living-dining room and about twelve feet wide. It had several seating arrangements scattered about, consisting of dining tables, chairs and serving carts. It looked an ideal setting for a party. There were also numerous flowering potted plants strategically placed so as not to block the view of the sea – and yet, give the impression that one was in a terraced garden.

Guy stared at the panoramic view of the sea, slowly turning his head from side to side. "It's magnificent, Tonio. And this terrace is an ideal place for parties, isn't it?"

"Yes, I have several large gatherings here each year. But as to the view, you have the same prospect of the sea from your apartment – only less expansive."

"That's true. It's a small terrace – in keeping with the size of the unit, but it does offer a great view."

"Why don't you sit wherever you like and I'll go get the appetizers."

Guy chose a small bistro table next to the decorative, pierced terrace railing, and sat in one of the two chairs beside it. Tonio returned quickly with a tray of Sicilian appetizers, and a clear glass pitcher filled with a pale liquid, in which chunks of fruit floated. "Is that white Sangria?" Guy asked.

"No, it's a fruit punch. I thought I'd save the alcohol for dinner – I'm serving wine, if you don't mind."

"That will be fine. I must confess that I believe I've drunk more alcohol during my time in Sicily than throughout my whole life – because wine is served with all the meals here."

"Yes – the Mediterranean way of life!" Tonio said with a laugh.

"But strangely, I have never been really drunk here, either."

"That's probably because the wine has always accompanied a hearty meal."

"I suppose so. Tell me, if you will, how did your family come to own this magnificent condo?"

Tonio poured out two glasses of punch, handed one to Guy and began, "Actually, *my* family developed Villa Paradiso – as a condominium."

"How interesting. What had it been before?"

"The private residence of local aristocracy – a Count and Countess. Their ancestors built the place in the mid-1800s. Old photographs indicate it was quite ornate, originally. The family's income was primarily derived from several farms in the surrounding countryside, which were populated by tenants. The last Count came to control the estate as a young man during the stock market mania of the 1920s. He sold off most of the family's real estate holdings and invested in the high-flying market. Many of his investments were in American corporations. I don't have to tell you what happened to the family's fortunes when the stock market crash occurred. Then came the Depression. By the time the Second World War had started, the Count was forced to rent out some rooms in this building in order to keep up with the maintenance and tax bills. His hope was that his only son – who was university-educated, would reverse the family's fortunes after the War. Unfortunately, the son was killed while serving on the battlefield. The Count and Countess went into physical and mental decline after the War – in grief over both their son and the loss of the family's wealth. Post-war housing was very tight in Italy, so they moved into a single large room and rented out every possible inch of space, in order to survive. In the meantime, no repairs were made, so the building became more and more decrepit. About twenty years ago, the Count and Countess were so ill they no longer could cope with such a responsibility. A religious Order of nursing nuns who run a home for the elderly over in Catania agreed to take them both in for lifelong care, provided they made an up-front endowment to the Order. Since they had no resources other than the Villa Paradiso, everything depended upon the successful sale of the property. My father was a building contractor at the time and heard about the property as soon as it came on the market. I remember him coming home and telling my mother, sister and me that he was determined to buy the property himself. He recognized it would re-quire extensive renovation, but thought it would guar-antee our family's future financial security. He envi-sioned creating an apartment home for us and rent-ing out the other units."

"But it's a *condominium*, isn't it?" Guy asked – fas-cinated, as usual, by stories of how individual families have managed to survive over the years.

"Yes – I'll get to that. Anyway, my father offered a price which was fair to the Count and Countess – it did allow them to meet the nuns' endowment requirements, but was also a bargain for us. Once my father took control of the property, he realized that renovations would be more costly and extensive than originally estimated, and that a rental complex would take too long to return his investment. So, he decided to incorporate the building as a condominium and sell off the other apartments."

"I see," Guy said, as he finished off the last of the appetizers. Tonio took this opportunity to take a long swig from his glass, before he continued with his story. But before he could speak again, Guy asked, "How many units are there in the building?"

"Six – but only four were sold to others by my father. This unit is the largest and most elaborate, and was to be our own home from the start. This floor also contains two one-bedroom units – the one you are renting, which has the choice sea view, and another which faces the courtyard and the street. Then on the ground floor are two two-bedroom units and the studio apartment the Marconis occupy. Originally, my father expected to sell the studio apartment also, but during the renovation process – which took several years, by the way – due to sporadic financing, he came to the conclusion that without an on-site portinari – I believe Americans prefer the French term, *concierge* — owners and tenants of the other units would be knocking on our door day and night with nuisance requests. So, he retained ownership of the studio unit also, and in the condominium by-laws each owner is assessed a monthly fee to cover the cost of on-site management by the portinari. Luckily,

Stefano and Irini are only the second couple we've had to hire in that role over the years."

"That makes a lot of sense. Who owns the other units?"

"The units have changed hands several times over the years, but usually they are owned by foreigners who come here once or twice a year on holiday, and rent out their unit to tourists when they are not in residence. That was another clever part of my father's plans. The by-laws also state that *our* real estate/property management firm must be the sole agent when a unit is rented or sold. At least we have first right of refusal to handle the property. In fact, the unit where you've been staying is going on the market soon after you vacate. At least, after I have had a chance to clean it and make any necessary repairs that will expedite the sale."

"Really? Why is it coming on the market?"

"The owners are elderly Belgians who used it for personal vacations and rental income for years. But, it's the same old story – they need cash for end-of-life care, due to diminished health."

"I see. I know absolutely *nothing* about property – I've always rented. In fact, I've been in the same small studio apartment for a decade now, back home. Just out of curiosity, what does something like my unit sell for in this market?"

"Well, the price hasn't been set yet. I have to inspect it and consult with the sellers. But, I guess I could give you a *rough* estimate of what I think it will be. Hum…you probably need a figure in U. S. dollars. I'm thinking in terms of Lira – but you know, we switch to the Euro shortly."

"Yes. I'm sure there will be extra paperwork for your office for quite some time – in view of such a major currency change."

"I'd say that the asking price on that one-bedroom unit will probably be in the range of about $140,000, in your currency."

"Wow!" Guy exclaimed.

"Do you think that's too much?"

"No. Sorry. I didn't mean to imply that. I'm sure it's a bargain – all things considered. But as someone who lives on a modest Associate Professor's salary, I'm just always amazed when I hear figures like that bandied about for *any* item – a Ferrari, a home, whatever."

"I understand. It occurs to me that you could be of considerable assistance if you could alert me to any problems with the unit which I ought to correct before trying to sell it."

Guy thought for several moments before responding. "Actually, it's in very good shape. There were two things that irritated me a bit, however. The faucets on the kitchen and bathroom sinks are very old-fashioned and frankly, I found them difficult to turn easily."

"The faucets. Well, they are an inexpensive item to replace. I'll check them out. Anything else?"

"The only other thing is probably cultural. I'm aware that the refrigerators in Taormina – in Europe as a whole, tend to be much smaller than in America. I'm sure this is because of the emphasis here on going to the market almost daily – as opposed to once a week as we do back home. So, a small refrigerator is the norm here – but I found it to be a nuisance during my stay. In fact, I even took the time to measure the space around it, and there is room for a unit that's at least a little bigger."

"I see. A larger refrigerator that will still fit in the allotted space. Okay, I'll check into that also. Let me know if you think of anything else." At that, Tonio glanced at his wristwatch. "I think we'd better eat soon. I've set the inside table for dinner, unless you prefer to eat on the terrace."

"Whichever you prefer. Although, to be honest with you, I'd love to have the chance to enjoy the ambiance of that beautiful large room."

"And so it will be! We'll eat indoors. Let's take these things into the kitchen, and you can help me bring the roasted veal and the rest to the table."

"Roasted veal?"

"Yes. I hope that's okay with you. I assumed that after nearly two months in Sicily, you've had your fill of fish for awhile."

"As much as I've enjoyed the fish, you're right – veal will be a welcome treat," Guy said, as he followed Tonio into the kitchen, carrying the empty appetizer tray and dirty plates.

Later, when they were halfway through their meal in the elegant living-dining room, Guy deliberately deflected questions Tonio raised about the depressing 9/11 tragedy — by asking *him* how his family came to be associated with the Baron.

"Ah," Tonio sighed, "that also is a long story – like the history of the Villa Paradiso."

Guy laughed, and said, "I've come to the conclusion that there are only *long* stories in Taormina!"

"All right – here goes," Tonio responded. "My grandfather and his brother were the sons of a poor fisherman. My great-grandfather didn't even have his own boat – just a fishing net, which my great-grandmother helped him keep in good repair. Unfortunately, his two sons were born with a deformed foot – like mine. It's apparently a genetic trait in our family, although it skipped my father's generation – and my sister. Anyway, my great-grandfather was lost at sea during a raging storm that capsized the boat he was working on, and before long, his wife went mad with fear and starvation – so she jumped off a cliff to join him in a watery grave. This left my grandfather and his brother as deformed, penniless orphans at the ages of eleven and twelve."

"How tragic!"

"It gets worse before it gets better," Tonio continued. "Taormina was filled with superstitious people then, who always viewed the foot deformities as punishment from God for centuries-old Valli family sins, so my Nonno and his brother were always mistreated and viewed as *cursed* by many of the local populace – even *before* their parents died. Now, as despised orphans, they were desperate. They were found by an elderly man and his wife, sleeping in a goat shed next to their one-room cottage one morning. This childless couple, who were having increasing difficulty tending their herd of goats, offered to let them sleep on a bed of straw in the goat shed, and give them regular meals, in exchange for tending the goats, milking them, making cheese and so forth."

"That must have seemed a Godsend to your Nonno and his brother!"

"It was. It truly was. Anyway, a few years later *your* grandfather – I forget his name..."

"Angelo Zambri."

"Yes – Angelo. He was the only local boy their age who had ever been kind to them. He had been posing for the Baron for some time, building an account to go to America. He convinced the Baron to visit them and determine if they would also be suitable models. Angelo and the Baron went to see them and the Baron was convinced their beauty could be captured on film. However, he would have to 'hide' their deformities. This was cleverly done by placing the twisted foot behind a prop or object – or just by careful cropping of the negative, before printing. Soon, my Nonno and his brother had accounts in their names at the Baron's bank. From the beginning, the Baron insisted that as soon as sufficient funds had accumulated, they should be fitted with special shoes which would allow them to walk normally, without their pronounced limps."

"I continue to be amazed at the Baron's concern for his models."

"Yes, the world will never know the full story. In this case, they had no shoes of *any* kind until the Baron arranged for a master shoemaker to come from Catania and measure their feet for customized shoes. The shoemaker suggested they be made a size larger, so they would last longer – since they were now teenagers who were growing rapidly."

"A wise decision. Did the Baron purchase the shoes for them?"

"He insisted the shoes be purchased with the money they earned from modeling. He felt they had to learn the values of thrift and careful spending, or they would dissipate any future funds which fell into their hands."

"Yes – I've heard other stories which underscore his concern that the poor youth of Taormina who posed for him learn the value of thrift."

"Anyway, the shoes eventually arrived in the mail, and as my Nonno told my father, who related the story to me – these shoes changed their lives completely. Now they could walk tall and proud, and over time, people who had previously been hostile became civil towards them – viewing them as 'normal'. It wasn't long after that that their elderly employers died in a horrible fire that suddenly broke out in the crumbling chimney of their little cottage while my Nonno and his brother were at the Baron's villa, posing. They were devastated that they weren't there at the time to rescue them – but some things are meant to be, are they not?"

"Yes" Guy replied, somberly. "I guess so."

"Somehow, most of the goats in the shed were rescued by passersby. My Nonno and his brother reinforced the shed with salvaged materials from the cottage fire, and stayed on the property until the local town notary approached them several weeks later with a short, signed document indicating their elderly, childless employers had left the property to them."

"You can't mean it!"

"Yes, I do. Without ever telling the lads, they apparently went to the notary and had this document drawn up and arranged for it to be kept in his office in town. Well, anyway, getting back to the Valli family saga – the inheritance of that small piece of land, and the modeling income from the Baron's photos, eventually was parlayed by Nonno and his brother into the room-by-room construction of a small inn, for travelers, on the property. It took a long time to complete the project, but some years later, that building and the land were sold in order to buy a more-valuable property in town. The brothers became builders, married local women, and had children. My father was an only child and Nonno's brother only had daughters. The family's income was stable enough for my father to finish high school and take a short course in bookkeeping. He helped my grandfather with his construction projects and eventually went into real estate sales, as well as construction. I took over the real estate business after taking some courses in Catania – where it *all* started, in some ways, years ago when the shoemaker came to Taormina."

By now, Guy had finished eating and had been sitting enraptured by this story. "I never cease to be amazed by these local rags-to-riches stories, which all seem to get back to the Baron at some point."

"Yes," Tonio reflected. "Our shared interest in male beauty and man-on-man love is not the *only* reason we exalt in the Brotherhood. The Baron also taught many of our ancestors how to gain pride in themselves and their accomplishments. But enough of history – we are in the here-and-now. Come, help me take these dirty dishes to the sink and I shall take you on the promised tour of the rest of the apartment."

"Great!" Guy exclaimed, as he started to clear the table.

After the dishes, pots and related dinner items were scraped and left to soak in soapy water in the kitchen sink, Tonio took Guy to the far end of the living-dining room, where the end wall abutted the apartment he was renting. "This is my sister's bedroom – much as she left it when she married."

Guy looked around the room, girlishly appointed with pink fabrics, gold-leaf furniture and lots of roses in the wallpaper. "I suspect she was your father's *princess*," Guy remarked.

"She was. She was. And it bothered me while I was growing up. I thought I could never please him, make him proud. But then, after he gradually related

the family history to me, and the Baron's contribu-
tion to our success, we started to become closer. I
was in total disbelief the night he told me about the
Brotherhood, and invited me to join. At my initiation, he stood proudly beside me in all my misshapen
nakedness, and I finally felt totally whole."

Guy realized this was a sensitive area for Tonio to
enter, so he added, "Obviously, you fulfilled all his
expectations, or he wouldn't have left you the business."

"That's true," Tonio replied, as he nervously
cleared his throat. "Anyway, my old bedroom is next
door – my nieces stay in it when they are here."

When Guy peeked into this second room, he saw
a nondescript "guest" bedroom, furnished neutrally
to satisfy a man or a woman. Tonio spoke up, "The
only change I really made was to replace my old
double bed with twin beds, as my nieces would never
share a bed. If you think their mother was a princess,
you should see these two!"

Guy laughed, as he followed Tonio out of the room
and into a bathroom which separated the two bedrooms, serving both. Guy loved the Italian tile, which
was used in considerable abundance in this bath – as
well as in the kitchen.

"Come – my room is on the other end. It's my
parents' former bedroom. I've kept their furniture and
just added some personal items and touches." When
they reached the carved double-doors on the other
end of the large living-dining room, Tonio threw them
open, using a grand gesture. He signaled for Guy to
enter ahead of him. Guy was speechless at first, as he
surveyed what obviously was a large master *suite*. The
main room served as the sleeping area. The enormous

bed was heavy and ornately carved. A huge armoire almost totally covered one whole wall. Tonio saw him staring at its intricate carved design and led him to it. He swung open the doors. Inside, Tonio had built a shrine. A large portrait of the Baron was in the center of the display. Old photographs of several naked youths were on either side. "My grandfather and his brother," he pointed out to Guy. And then, in a less-prominent position were photos of himself and his father – obviously taken for the archives of the Brotherhood. Tonio struck a match and lit the votive candle which stood before the Baron's photograph. After a few moments of respectful contemplation, he directed Guy to an adjoining sitting area – similar to an alcove. Several large, comfortable chairs were placed along one wall, while on the opposite wall there was an open unit holding a television, video player, stereo, dual speakers and related electronics.

"I assume these electronics are some of the *personal* touches you added to this suite – along with the shrine."

"Yes. I have an extensive video and CD collection, and spend much of my precious free time here. But look, come into the bath – this is where my parents splurged when they built this apartment."

Tonio ushered Guy into the largest private bathroom he'd ever seen. Italian marble and tile were everywhere. In addition to a matching toilet and bidet, a separate shower, double sinks and a vanity area – the room contained a huge marble tub with multiple faucets.

"Wow!" Guy exclaimed, as he rushed to the tub and sat on its wide ledge.

"I can spend hours in here," Tonio said, "when I have the time. It's also a shrine to the Baron – look!"

At that, Tonio took a decorative folding screen that stood in one corner and turned it around. On the other side were enlargements of photos taken by von Gloeden. "Your cousin, Luca, made these for me, and a local cabinetmaker – a Brother of course, created the screen. Sometimes I lie in the tub and stare at it, while I pleasure myself."

"The whole room is wonderfully decadent!" Guy laughed.

Tonio let Guy explore the room for a few more moments and then he said, "Would you take some photos of me? For the archives? Luca will gladly develop any film the Brothers submit to him."

Guy hesitated a moment, then said, "You mean *nude*?"

"Yes.

"Well, if you like."

At that, Tonio walked back to the sitting room alcove and took a camera from one of the shelves. It had obviously been pre-loaded with film. He then started to strip and place his clothes over a chair. Guy watched in fascination as Tonio got down to his orthopedic shoe – which, once removed, transformed his body so that he now was in a continual *contrapposto* pose. Guy recalled the many Classical male nude statues he'd seen where the torso balances on just one leg, creating a pleasing "S" curve to the body. This is what he now saw in the nude Tonio. Tonio looked up at Guy expectantly. His gold medallion glistened on his smooth chest. He maintained a smile and gazed directly into Guy's eyes for a few seconds – until Guy realized he was waiting for him to strip too. Guy smiled, shrugged his shoulders a bit, and followed suit. When they were both naked, Tonio handed Guy the camera and asked him to take over the photo shoot. Guy remembered the Baron's photos of Tonio's ancestors, with their deformed feet out of camera range, and so he had Tonio sit on the edge of the marble tub, with his "damaged" foot inside the tub – out of sight. Guy adjusted Tonio's other leg so there would be a clear view of his crotch, and placed his arms in a position to highlight the sensuous nature of the pose. As he made these preparations, he noticed Tonio had a modest cock, with a neat pubic bush the same color as his eyes and the hair on his head. Guy then took several pictures from different angles.

"And you?" Tonio inquired. "The same?"

"Okay," Guy said, as he positioned himself on the edge of the tub to be photographed. After Tonio took several pictures of him, he handed back the camera to Guy and stood in the tub with his back to the camera. At this point Guy fully appreciated Tonio's *beautiful* ass, made more tempting by the S-shaped curve to his body, due to his deformity. Guy entered the tub and placed Tonio's hands against the wall. Then he positioned Tonio's body so the pose would emanate maximum eroticism. As he touched Tonio's buttocks, to position them to his liking, he heard a soft moan escape his model's lips. Guy realized this was obviously a very erogenous zone for his new friend.

After several pictures were taken, they switched places again, and when Tonio had finished photographing Guy, he put the camera back on the shelf. Then he took Guy silently by the hand and led him to the large, separate glass shower on one end of the huge bathroom. He adjusted the water temperature and began to soap Guy all over. Guy reciprocated.

Soon, their bodies were rubbing against each other and they were tongue kissing. Tonio was shorter and smaller in stature than Guy, requiring Guy to lean down a bit. All the while, Tonio clung to him like a needy child. After they toweled each other off, Tonio led him from the bathroom, through the sitting room alcove and to the gigantic bed. He pulled back the covers, jumped in, and beckoned to Guy to join him. After he was firmly locked in Guy's arms, he said, "I have a full sex life, despite my ugly foot, because the Brothers are generous. Even though we all worship the ideal male body, the Brothers recognize that all men are beautiful – in their own way. Respect is shown to all during the Revels. Those who are usually alone on their mats pleasuring themselves are there because it is their preference. And we all respect that. Some are content to be voyeurs and get off on the orgy around them. That is all right with the Brothers. For myself, I crave regular physical communion, with men, of the type Roberto Rossi provided at your initiation. Would you honor me in the same way tonight?"

It took Guy a moment or two to remember that Roberto took Tonio from behind, doggie-style, that night. "Um….I'm not really into anal activity, Tonio. I fear giving pain, or receiving it."

"It will not be painful for me. You saw me take Roberto's horse-cock with ease that night. In truth, he massaged me many times over the years with his fingers and dildos – after hours in his surgery, so I could fully enjoy being entered."

Guy looked up at the ceiling while he thought about Tonio's request.

"If you're concerned about safe sex, here – look," Tonio said, as he reached over to the nearby nightstand and pulled open a drawer filled with devices and disease-prevention supplies.

Guy chuckled, "That's *another* feature of the Brotherhood – 'be prepared'. I swear, you're just a group of grown-up Boy Scouts!"

"We *are* a group of...how do you say...*Scouts*," Tonio laughed, in return. "Don't count yourself out, now that you've been initiated."

At that, Guy hugged and kissed Tonio until he was sufficiently aroused to dress his cock with one of the nearby condoms. Tonio instructed him on how and where to use the lube and guided Guy's cock into his hot, wet, gaping hole. This was a new experience for Guy. The initial heat of Tonio's body surprised him, and along with the pressure on his dick, drove him wild. He came quicker than usual, and apologized to Tonio. "I'm sorry. I should have prolonged your pleasure, Tonio."

In between gasps for air, Tonio replied, "It was wonderful. Don't worry. And my pleasure isn't over yet."

Tonio then swung around and dressed his rigid cock with a condom. He then pushed it into Guy's face. Guy eagerly pleasured this sweet man, and after Tonio came, they lay in each other's arms for almost an hour. When Guy started to rise to dress and return to his apartment, Tonio pulled him back into the bed. "Stay, stay the night. You have only to cross the courtyard tomorrow morning – in order to go back to your place."

• EIGHTEEN •

"Would you like some grapes or figs?" Luca asked – offering the plastic container they were in to Guy. The two of them were sitting on the grass, overlooking the ruins of the Roman Amphitheater in Siracusa.

"No thanks, I'm full. Maybe later, in the car," Guy replied, as he scattered bread crumbs from his napkin in the grass, for birds to find later.

They had left Taormina right on schedule early in the morning and had already toured Siracusa's main sights – including the Greek Theater, the cave known as Dionysus's Ear, and several temple ruins. Guy took slides at each stop, in hopes of using them one day in art history lectures.

"Theresa packed a delicious lunch, Luca. Be sure to tell her when you return home."

"She'll be glad to hear that. She does take pride in her cooking. She reminded me, while she was preparing the food this morning, that *this* trip is the kind of thing we've promised ourselves after I retire."

"Are you thinking of retiring soon?"

"We figure in about five years. By then the twins will be through with college and we won't have any more major expenses associated with raising them."

"What will you do? Won't you miss the shop?"

"Ha!" Luca laughed. "My business has been deteriorating for at least a decade. Think of it – every-

thing I do there has been affected by technology –
the kind that takes customers away from me – so that
my revenues drop monthly. Photo-developing and film
sales dropped when tourists started showing up with
video recorders. Now, they have digital cameras. I still
develop film for a few locals and some tourists who
want to see their 35 mm pictures right away – one-
hour service. But, even some of the locals are sending
pictures back and forth over the internet now."

"What about the books and stationery?"

"Same thing. People are buying books over the
internet, so I stopped stocking popular fiction and
nonfiction titles. Everything I offer now is for tourists – sightseeing books on Sicily and Taormina, and
the little von Gloeden volume we've sold for years.
As for stationery and greeting cards – lots of people
use email instead of them, so I just have postcards
for the tourists. If I can last five *more* years, I'll consider myself lucky."

"What will you do? Where will you go?"

"Our choices are limited. We don't have large savings. It took just about everything we could earn to
pay off the mortgage and raise the twins. However,
Tonio Valli assures us we will have a very nice nest
egg to supplement my modest pension when we eventually sell our place on the Corso."

"I'm sure that property has escalated in value over
the years."

"It has. And even though it's small, if the pur-
chaser doesn't want to live in the upstairs apartment,
it can be used to expand the shop below."

"Won't it be expensive for you to buy a retirement home?"

"We're covered there. Theresa's parents owned a
three-bedroom apartment in Naxos – Theresa's

widowed mother and her sister live there now. After my father-in-law died, Theresa's mother put the deed in her two daughters' names – with lifetime tenancy for herself. When I retire, we'll move into the third bedroom. By then, Theresa's sister will likely be living there alone – her mother is quite elderly and in poor health, and we *are* talking about five years in the future."

"Won't you miss Taormina? Roberto? The Brotherhood?"

"Naxos is just a short distance away. I'll have plenty of time to go back and forth. Theresa and her sister will be preoccupied with each other. If I can't set up a darkroom in the apartment, Roberto will make space for one in his surgery, so I can continue the work of the Brotherhood."

"Well, it sounds like you have your future all mapped out."

"I wish that were so, but there are many other unresolved issues. Good God! Look at the time! I want to get you to Piazza Armerina while the site is still open for touring this afternoon – so we'd better go."

Guy and Luca quickly gathered up the picnic items and were soon heading West toward Piazza Armerina – arriving in time to visit the fabulous Villa Romana, with its 60,000 square feet of incredible Roman mosaics. The latter represented hunting scenes, imaginary creatures, landscapes, and Guy's two favorites: bikini-clad young women exercising in much the same way as people do today, and a wonderfully homoerotic scene of a slave boy tending to his naked master in the bath. The guards were announcing the closing of the site at sunset, just as Guy and Luca were making their way back to the car park. Luca had a list of pensiones in the area and they quickly found one on the road to Agrigento – the Valley of the Temples, which they planned to visit the following morning.

Later that night, after they returned to the pensione from dinner in a nearby restaurant, they showered, got in bed, and snuggled for a while before Guy made a movement to go down on Luca. Luca parried Guy's movement by getting into position for sixty-nine. For some time, they reveled in the joy of their man-love, knowing they would soon be parting for a long time – possibly forever. Afterwards, Guy fell asleep in Luca's arms.

Late the next morning, they arrived at Agrigento. Guy was overwhelmed by the sight of so many well-preserved Greek temples. Luca's guidebook explained that many were believed to be misnamed. As new archeological evidence emerged, there was reason to believe that some of the traditional names of these temples were more *fanciful* than historically accurate. Still, Guy was thrilled to be photographing edifices with such lofty names as: The Temple of Hercules, The Tomb of Theron, The Temple of Aesculapius, The Temple of Concord – and of course, The Temple of Olympian Zeus.

The visit to Agrigento was so mind-boggling that Guy didn't speak for several kilometers after he and Luca were back on the road, heading North, in the direction of Palermo.

"Are you all right?" Luca asked.

"Yes, just over-whelmed. I hope these slides come out. They'll be great for use in class."

"I gave you the best slide film I carry in my shop, so if there's a problem, it's likely to be with the *photographer*!" Luca said, with a laugh.

After a while, Guy settled down and turned the conversation to the twins' college plans.

"Well," Luca responded to Guy's query, "they're applying now for next Fall, since they graduate high school in the Spring."

"What do they want to study?"

"They're both obsessed with computers. Mario thinks he wants to be a software engineer and Dario is interested in computer art, computer graphics."

"I see. Can they study that in Taormina?"

"No. The nearest school would be in Catania. But they are also applying to schools in Palermo."

"I'm sure you'll miss them."

"Roberto and I are already discussing that. Fredo wants to follow in his father's footsteps. He will probably do his pre-medical work somewhere in Sicily, but for medical school, he will likely go to the mainland – Rome, Naples, Bologna. Roberto and I are very close to our sons, so it will be difficult, but it is the way of life. And, we can 'console' each other after they leave – we have that, at least."

"I suppose that when the boys are old enough to join the Brotherhood, you will grow even closer."

"*If* they join. Remember, it is strictly voluntary. In fact, they will each be approached *separately* – even the twins. At some point after their twenty-first birthdays, Roberto and I will engage them in general discussions of the Baron's work. They are already familiar with it, living in Taormina and also seeing the von Gloeden book we sell in the shop. Then each one who appears comfortable with the subject will be shown some of the archival photos, and if he still seems receptive, will be told of his ancestors who posed for the Baron – and shown pictures of them. If he appears proud of this family connection, then at some point he will be told of the Brotherhood and invited to undergo examination and orientation with Roberto."

"So, it's really a multi-stage process."

"Yes — you went through it yourself, only it was greatly expedited because of your age and circumstances."

"So, you're not automatically assuming all three will want to join?"

"No. Times have changed. We're finding increasing lack of interest among young people today. Many have no appreciation for history. Also, they want to leave town for the 'big city', as soon as possible. It's also more and more difficult for an Italian man to find a wife who would be content to stay at home and bear him sons – for the next generation of Brothers. Italian women are pursuing careers as never before. Have you seen our birth rates in Italy – they're *very* low!"

"I hadn't thought of all that. I just figured the Brotherhood would go on forever."

"Even in the worst case scenario, it will last for some years, in view of the current membership. However, Roberto and I do get depressed when we think that our long-held dream may not come to pass."

"What dream is that?"

"That all three boys agree to join and are driven to Pietro Stanza's farm in separate cars on the night of their initiation. That they encounter each other there, experiencing as much joy as we. Then during the Revels after the initiation ceremony, we envision Mario, Dario and Fredo retiring to a nearby mat and making love to each other, in the presence of their new-found Brothers. Roberto and I have been aware, for years, they've been engaging in such activity since early adolescence – as we did. And we hope their mutual love will be as enduring as ours."

"And you two will be on a nearby mat, expressing your love openly."

"Yes."

"Hopefully, that will serve as an example to them."

"Hopefully."

Luca drove in silence for another hour, obviously pre-occupied with thoughts stirred up by this conversation. Then, he bolted upright and said, "Yes – there it is!"

They pulled into the courtyard of a quaint country inn. It was on the list he had brought with him. After checking in for the night, he and Guy had an early dinner in the beautiful walled garden at the back. When they returned to their room, Luca got out his roadmap. "Tomorrow, we'll head to Monreale, on this side of Palermo. There's something I want to show you there. Then, we'll spend the rest of the day sightseeing in Palermo before we go to our hotel. I made the Palermo hotel reservation in advance, to be sure we had a place to stay on your last night. This is a hotel on the water – Roberto and I stayed there once, and I think you'll like it."

"Everything sounds great. It looks like we'll get a lot done on my last day in Sicily."

"Yes. But for now, I'm exhausted from the driving. I just want to take a shower and go to bed. Do you mind if I use that tiny shower first, Guy?"

"Not at all – go ahead."

Later, after Guy emerged from the shower and dried himself off, he looked down at Luca, lying naked on the bed, face down.

"You know, a full-body massage might loosen up some of those tight muscles and help you drive more comfortably tomorrow," Guy whispered in Luca's left ear.

"Ah, but where is there someone to provide such service?" Luca replied.

"Oh, Lord Zeus, Ganymede is here – not only with your wine cup, but also with scented oils to massage your sacred body."

"Then I command you to show homage to your Lord!"

Guy obediently massaged the whole of Luca's back, starting at the neck and working down to his toes. When he parted his buttocks to work each check separately, Luca's balls appeared. He avoided them for the time being, knowing he would have them at his disposal after he flipped his cousin over on his back.

"Lord, permit me to turn your sacred body over, so I may worship your glorious chest."

Luca heaved a sigh and rolled over. His eyes were closed. Guy started massaging him behind his ears. Then, his neck. Then his smooth chest – where there were so few gray chest hairs, they could have been easily counted. When he reached Luca's nipples, they were already erect. He gently kissed them, one-by-one. He saved the crotch for last, going instead to the thighs – right first, and then the left. After he finished massaging and kissing Luca's feet, he placed his hands on his cousin's crotch. Luca was already erect. Guy reached for a condom from his toilet kit on the nightstand, dressed this godly man's cock, and pleasured him with his hungry mouth. After Luca exploded in ecstasy, Guy started to rise, but Luca pulled him back down, saying, "And now, Ganymede, Zeus will reward his beloved cupbearer."

When Guy's travel alarm went off the next morning, he couldn't move. Luca had him locked in a tight embrace. His arms were around Guy's chest, his legs around his torso. Guy had to shake him awake in order to extricate himself. Luca laughed at the situation, and they made light of the previous evening's events as they shaved and dressed. After a continental breakfast at the inn, they loaded up the car and continued North, toward Monreale.

For Guy, Monreale's cathedral and cloister were a marvel! The complex's Arab-Norman-Romanesque style, with varying column and capital designs – often covered with gold leaf and mosaics, was truly unique. He would have liked to have stayed longer, but Luca pointed out that they must descend the hill into Palermo for lunch and an afternoon of sightseeing. After the car was left in a centrally-located Palermo car park, they spent the afternoon visiting the Archeological Museum, Modern Art Museum and the Garibaldi House – but not before eating lunch at an outdoor café near the English Garden.

The ride to their hotel later took only a few minutes. The check-in process went quickly and after dropping their luggage in the room, Luca suggested they go out for gelati and a visit to quaint Lincoln Park, which was next door to the hotel. "There are interesting mosaics in the park which you will enjoy, Guy."

The park was serene, overlooking the bay. A few young children were running around, tended by adults.

"Well," Luca said, turning to Guy as they sat on a park bench facing the water, "at least you now have a taste of Sicily – beyond Taormina."

"Oh, Luca, this has been a *wonderful* way to end my stay here."

"There is much, much more to see in Sicily, but perhaps the next time....."

"Yes," Guy said, "perhaps the next time."

Luca looked off into the distance and Guy sensed he was debating with himself about what to say next. "You look like you have something on your mind, Luca."

Luca cleared his throat, nervously, in a momentary show of embarrassment. Then he said, "I was just wondering.....I mean, you have such a healthy appetite for sex, how will you manage in America to keep the Brotherhood's vow of celibacy outside the group?"

Guy chuckled. "You know, at the time I talked with Dr. Rossi about all that, I didn't completely consider the long-term implications. However, I *was* celibate for over a year before I came here. I had gotten tired of what seemed to be endless superficial relationships and mean-spiritedness in the gay world around me. I'm not sure how to describe it to you Luca – but in America, *youth* is worshipped. And young men know they have power over people my age. They are quick to dismiss us as decrepit – unless they want to exploit us for money, gifts. Relationships often wind up being very superficial, and there are many petty jealousies as aging 'queens' fight over these narcissistic youths. That's why I am so impressed with the Brotherhood. While much of the Baron's work celebrated the timeless beauty of the ephebe, the Broth-

ers still respect *all* men – of all shapes, sizes and ages.
No one acts proprietary and expects monogamy of
those to whom he may have a special attraction. As
long as the Brotherhood as a whole is generating love
among its members, happiness abounds. The love
among the Brothers is so free, so pervasive, so un-
shackled by Puritan convention, that I sometimes
believe I must have dreamed all this."

"But how will you handle your sex drive when
the Brothers are no longer around?"

"Masturbation – and plenty of it. Pornography is
everywhere today, and I have a vivid imagination and
fantasy life. *Now*, I can add memories of the Brotherhood to my fantasy life – my initiation rite, the archival photos, you, Roberto, Father Leonardo, Tonio
Valli."

"Father Leonardo? Tonio Valli? Are you saying…"

"Yes. I assumed they had already told you."

"No – but I'm delighted our family satyr from
America has so quickly *blended* with the Brotherhood.
Did Father Leonardo 'happen' the day you went to
the parish house to do genealogical research?"

"Yes. *He* initiated it, but I gladly participated."

"Do you know about his sibling – also a priest
and a Brother?"

"Oh yes – with the same hypnotic green eyes, as I
recall from my initiation, when they came through
the receiving line to congratulate me."

"A three-way with them is the thrill-of-a-lifetime,
Cousin."

"And have you been so thrilled, Luca?"

"Twice! But tell me of Tonio."

"I think *your* story about the green-eyed Brothers
would be much more interesting, but since you

asked.....I told you Tonio invited me to dinner last week?"

"Yes."

"Well, afterwards, he suggested we take some photographs of each other for the Brotherhood's archives. He said he'd bring the film to you to develop. I gather he hasn't."

"No. He's very busy with his many business ventures. Also, did he know we were taking this trip?"

"Yes."

"Then he may have been afraid to leave it with the twins or Theresa – they all develop film in the shop."

"Of course. Anyway, he invited me to have sex with him and stay the night."

"And you did."

"Yes – but he wanted *anal* sex and I've never been into *that*."

"So you refused?"

"No. He told me a long story of how Roberto used massage and dildos to help him accommodate a man's cock, and finally convinced me that I need have no fear of hurting him."

"Was *that* your main concern – *hurting* him? It wasn't AIDS or something else?"

"No. We were going to be using condoms, so I guess I wasn't concerned about disease. It was the pain issue. From the first time I ever had sex with a man, I refused to be entered or to enter anyone else, because I couldn't imagine anything more painful."

"But people have anal sex *all* the time – there must be something pleasurable about it – yes?"

"So I've been told. I certainly noticed, at my initiation, that Tonio seemed to be in ecstasy while

Roberto plowed him on the mat next to ours."

"Let me tell you a little about Tonio, Guy. Even though he worked with his father for most of his life, there was a distance between them for many years. Tonio felt his father was too strict and demanding of him, while favoring his sister. That all changed when Tonio was old enough to be initiated into the Brotherhood. After that, father and son became very close. They finally started to really share their feelings and Tonio learned that his father decided at his birth that Tonio would grow up to be an 'emotional cripple' if he were shown too much sympathy over his deformed foot. So, he showed him no special treatment, and in fact may have gone overboard a bit – applying too much pressure at times. The end result, though, was that Tonio grew up to be independent and strong-willed, and not prone to self-pity. He's a very astute businessman who has increased the family fortunes greatly."

"Yes – I gathered that. When I called to tell him I would be vacating the apartment early, his first concern was whether I was expecting a rebate on the rent!"

"That's Tonio – watches *every* penny. But he is fair and honest. Anyway, when his Papa died, he fell apart. He wound up at Roberto's surgery night after night. Roberto prescribed antidepressants, but the most effective treatment he rendered appeared to be his simple willingness to listen to Tonio discussing his relationship with his father. Anyway, eventually Tonio got around to discussing his sex life with the Brothers and his inability to tolerate anal sex because of the pain. He asked Roberto for help, and for a time Roberto massaged him internally, got him used to dildos of varying size – until one night Tonio pleaded with Roberto to take him with his horse-cock. He reasoned that if he could take Roberto, he was ready for anyone. The first attempt was awkward and a bit painful, but with practice, it has become Tonio's greatest pleasure in life – besides making money, of course! And, Roberto and many of the other Brothers are happy to accommodate him – even though anal sex is not that common within the Brotherhood."

"Yes – Roberto told me that during my medical examination in his office. That's why I was so surprised to see him engaging in it with Tonio on the night of my initiation."

"Consider it an act of Christian charity on Roberto's part – for a poor soul in distress," Luca laughed heartily. Guy joined him in the laughter, startling a young child going past them, being pushed in his stroller by his mother.

"And you," Luca asked, "did you enjoy being the active partner at Tonio's? Or was it painful?"

Guy thought a moment. "It made my dick feel very hot – burning from his body temperature. But the pressure his rectum placed all around my organ was wonderful, and made me come quickly. Once I was convinced that he was in no real pain, I relaxed and enjoyed the *ride* – as they say."

"There you go. Life often offers opportunities for new experiences – to the adventurous."

Later, after they had eaten dinner in the hotel dining room, Guy suggested they retire early. He wanted to rearrange the items in his luggage one last time before his flight in the morning, and was already tired from a full day of sightseeing. He also wanted Luca rested before he drove back to Taormina after dropping him off at the Palermo Airport tomorrow.

They decided Luca would shower first, while Guy repacked. As Luca was walking toward the bathroom in all his naked glory, he pulled a gift-wrapped package from the little duffle bag he'd brought on this trip — so his small car trunk could accommodate Guy's multiple bags, and said, "Here, a little farewell gift."

Guy took the package like an eager child. "Why thank you, Luca. But it is *I* who should be giving *you* gifts."

"Enjoy," Luca said, with a smile, as he walked toward the shower.

Guy sat down and tore open the wrapping. He held in his hands a beautiful photo album of burgundy leather, with gold tooling. Stamped on the front, in gold letters, were the words *Memories of Taormina*. Upon opening the album, he found a dozen photos of Taormina, obviously taken by Luca. The scenes were gorgeous – all the famous sites, as well as the Villa Paradiso and Luca's shop on the Corso.

When Luca emerged from the shower, dripping wet, Guy rushed up to him and embraced him without waiting for him to dry off. "Thank you, thank you, for such a beautiful gift, Luca!"

"You're welcome. But it holds a secret. Wait a moment until I can dry off."

After Luca was dry, he sat on the bed and held the album in his naked lap. "See here, something to fool the customs inspectors and their obsession with pornography."

He then slowly pulled each photo out of the plastic-covered frame in which it lay, revealing an archival Brotherhood photo *behind* each of the Taormina scenes. There were the pictures he had secretly shown

Guy of Angelo, Rocco and Amadeo – taken by the Baron so many years ago, as well as the photos Luca, Roberto and Guy took at Pietro Stanza's during their Photo Expedition picnic. "Perhaps these will help stimulate you when you are back in America pleasuring yourself and thinking of your Taormina adventure," he said to Guy, with a smile.

Guy was delighted! "Luca, Luca," he murmured, as he viewed the precious photos. "I don't know what to....." His sentence was interrupted by Luca pushing his tongue down his throat. After a few minutes of deep kissing, Luca slapped him on the ass and said, "Get in there and take a shower, so we can go to bed. I'll replace the Taormina scenes in the album while you're in the bathroom."

Guy jumped off the bed, quickly stripped, and obediently headed for the shower, in anticipation of their last night of love-making. When they were finally settled in bed, locked in each other's arms, Guy said to Luca, "Earlier in the park, you asked me about my sex life. May I ask you a question about *yours*?"

"Of course. We need never keep secrets from each other."

"Well, as a single gay man, who obviously has no sexual interest in women, I've not quite understood how so many of the Brothers can be *husbands* – including you and Roberto."

"Ah, yes. Well, every man has his own story of course. But Roberto and I have similar ones. We were friends from primary school and when we entered adolescence we naturally experimented sexually with one another. However, it proved to be more than sex – it was love, deep and true love. We knew *that* by the time we graduated high school. Over the next few years, we focused on our chosen careers and were initiated into the Brotherhood, where we were allowed to openly express our love before our male relatives and the other Brothers. It went on that way for years – until we were in our late thirties and realized we would never have the chance of siring sons to follow us in preserving the Baron's legacy if we didn't marry. And so, we jointly sought women who would likely provide a home and family, while we continued our secret life and mutual love."

"But.....I hate to say this because it sounds judgmental – didn't it seem dishonest, in terms of your wedding vows?"

"Roberto and I both experienced guilt in the early years of marriage, but it was abated when we fathered sons. We took their births as 'signs' that we had gone down the proper path. Then too, from time-to-time the Brotherhood has arranged lectures on sexuality for the members. There are several psychologists who've belonged over the years. The one who currently is a member is a professor over in Catania and only gets to meetings occasionally. His viewpoint is that all humans are essentially bisexual, so our ability to seek pleasure with women *and* men is normal. One thing he said during a lecture several years ago has always stayed in my mind. One of the members told him he was concerned over the fact that while he received pleasure from sex with his wife *and* the Brothers, he definitely preferred sex with men. Since this is the view of most of the married Brothers, everyone eagerly leaned forward to hear the professor's reply. He said, very quietly, very simply, "Remember Brothers, the relationship between God the Father and *Adam* preceded the relationship between Adam and *Eve*. For some reason, that thought has always stayed with me. Have I answered your question?"

"Yes you have, Luca."

"Good, then I have one for you. Do you want our last night to be *special*?"

"Of course."

"Then I ask you to allow me to be the first man to *enter* you."

Guy pulled back from Luca's embrace. "Enter me? But I told you I fear the pain."

"Yes, but Roberto has schooled me well on how to prepare your manhole to receive me. I promise you, I shall be careful, gentle and go very slow. At any point, I will stop immediately, if you are uncomfortable."

Guy stared into Luca's beautiful, soft gray eyes. He owed this man *so* much. His cousin had introduced him to a whole new, secret world and had changed his life forever. How could he deny him this final pleasure?

"I trust you, Luca. Tell me what to do."

Luca went into the bathroom and brought back a dry bath towel. "Here, place this on the bed to protect the sheet and lie face down on it."

While Guy did this, Luca pulled a small container from his duffle bag, filled with condoms, lube and rubber gloves. "Now, close your eyes, Guy and *relax*. The more relaxed you are, the less discomfort."

Soon, Guy felt Luca's gloved and lubed fingers caressing his anus and exploring the opening. He giggled because it tickled more than hurt. As Luca talked to him softly, he explored deeper and deeper and wider and wider. Finally, he felt the time for entry had come. With a well-lubricated condom, he gradually inched his way in. Guy gasped softly with each centimeter of progress Luca made, until the latter was fully inside him. Then Luca started the gentle, rhythmic thrusts. Soon, Guy was experiencing a level of stimulation he'd never known before. Then Luca pulled him up on his knees and the thrusts became even deeper.

"Oh sweet Angelo, my brother," Luca whispered in a strange voice, "I fear I shall never see you again when you go to America."

Guy turned his head toward Luca and said, "Angelo? But I'm....."

"Yes, yes, my brother Angelo, this is our last time, I fear."

Guy was confused, but suddenly remembered the reading with Martin Francis in New York, which had played such a role in his decision to come to Sicily, and so he responded, "Rocco, my brother, I shall remember this *forever.*"

Guy exploded all over the bath towel moments before he felt Luca's shuddering orgasm inside his body. They both collapsed on the bed. Luca delayed withdrawing as long as he could, and then cleaned them both up before wrapping Guy in his arms for the night.

"Did that hurt as much as you feared, Guy?"

"No, Luca – you were magnificent. You gave me more pleasure than pain."

"Roberto has taught me well, I guess."

"Why did you call me 'Angelo'?"

"I didn't."

"Yes, Luca – you called me 'Angelo' twice, so I responded to you as if you were Rocco, his brother."

"Are you sure?"

"Yes. You said I was going to America and this was our last night together."

"But you are, and it is! I think you got carried away during the ecstasy of your first anal penetration!"

"No – it was real. Do you think the spirits of our grandfathers were here with us during those moments?'

"Cousin – *where* is this coming from?"

"Well, I told you about the reading with Martin Francis, where Nonno Angelo urged me to come to Sicily."

"Yes, but this is getting a little weird, isn't it?"

"I guess so."

"Let's forget all that and just enjoy our last night's embraces. Guy, Luca, Angelo, Rocco, Amadeo — and all the other Zambri men can occupy this bed tonight, at least in *spirit*. But only you and I shall occupy it *in the flesh*. Now, kiss me goodnight, my imaginative cousin!"

In the morning, after they were shaved, dressed and had stacked their luggage near the door, Luca and Guy looked into each other's eyes. They knew they would not be able to *properly* say 'goodbye' in public at the airport, so they rushed into each other's arms. Their tongues probed each other's throats. When they finally disengaged, Guy knelt before Luca, unzipped his cousin's fly, pulled out his cock, and kissed his magnificent Zambri foreskin. He reached into his shirt and pulled out his Brotherhood medallion, and pressed it against Luca's cock-head. Luca then pulled Guy to his feet and knelt down. He took Guy's cock from his unzipped pants, kissed *his* foreskin, and pressed his Brotherhood medallion against it. After he stood up, he offered his medallion to Guy to kiss. Guy did so, and then offered his medallion to Luca to kiss. After one last deep French kiss, they collected the luggage and headed for the elevator.

A half-hour later, when Luca dropped Guy and his bags off at the airport terminal, they shook hands on the sidewalk and softly said "good-bye" – as a porter approached Guy and offered assistance.

· NINETEEN ·

Dulles Airport looks like an armed camp! Guy thought, as he counted the number of gun-toting civilian and military personnel encircling deplaning passengers as they attempted to clear Customs. His belongings were given a very thorough going-over, but the customs agent paid little attention to the Taormina album with its secreted Brotherhood photos.

As Guy pushed his luggage cart toward Ground Transportation, he passed television sets spewing bits of information, all obviously related to 9/11 – *World Trade Center.....Ground Zero.....Taliban.....Al-Qaeda......*

At Ground Transportation, he spotted a driver holding a cardboard sign with *Zambri* written on it with black ink. He approached the driver and said, "I think you're looking for me."

As they walked to the car, they passed more armed guards. The driver noticed Guy staring at them and said, "It's a good thing that your flights were in and out of Dulles, Sir. Reagan was closed after 9/11 for fear of planes flying over the center of the District, and it's been a nightmare trying to do business over there since you left on your trip."

"It was just a matter of chance. I wanted a *direct* flight to Rome and I would have had to make a connection if I'd gone out of Reagan Airport."

When Guy was settled in the back seat of the car, the driver started to fill him in on what had happened at the Pentagon on 9/11, the increased security *and* inconvenience in D.C. now, the drop in tourism, and related frustrations. They had to make several detours on the way to his apartment on Connecticut Avenue, because certain areas near key government buildings were still off-limits. Guy finally just closed his eyes and sat quietly through it all, grateful that several months ago he had arranged with this car service to take him back and forth to Dulles. He only had to send a return confirmation by email from Taormina last week to be sure a driver was waiting for him this morning.

When they reached his apartment building, he asked for help getting his bags as far as the elevator. He had five – two with clothes, one with his manuscript and the reference books he needed while writing during his Sabbatical, another with his laptop, and a small carry-on with toiletries, camera and film. When all the bags were loaded onto the elevator, he gave the driver a generous tip and proceeded up to his floor.

The first thing that struck Guy as he entered his small studio apartment was how *fresh* it smelled, after being unoccupied for two months. Then he noticed a note on the kitchen counter:

Guy – I had my Nicaraguan cleaning lady dust your place, spray air freshener and run the A/C yesterday, in anticipation of your return. It's all part of your "birthday package". The rest will be delivered when I see you Saturday night. Welcome home and call – Chad

What a sweet friend he is! Guy thought. Then he remembered his last-minute purchase of a gift for Chad, at the Rome Airport Duty-Free Shops. He had found three beautiful Italian silk ties, in colors that coordinated with Chad's wardrobe, during the hour and one-half layover for his Dulles flight, after arriving in Rome from Palermo. He was glad he hadn't succumbed to the temptation to buy him a tacky souvenir in Sicily earlier, which surely would have clashed with Chad's carefully-appointed Art Deco condo near Dupont Circle.

Next to Chad's note were two piles of mail. The larger one consisted of magazines, journals, advertisements – items not worth forwarding to Italy. The smaller one contained several important letters which had arrived within the past week, too late to forward to Italy, in view of Guy's imminent return. Guy glanced at the return addresses on the envelopes in the latter group and opened one from the trust company in New Brunswick which had been administering the Trust Nonno Angelo left him. It was another reminder from Austin Walker, the current trustee, that Guy needed to come see him and arrange to take over control of the Trust, as per Nonno Angelo's Will, due to his having reached his fortieth birthday. Guy made a note to call Walker the next morning and arrange for a meeting next week, if possible.

Guy then went over to the small hutch near the dining area, reached up to the top shelf and removed a small round metal container. He sat in his favorite chair, holding Nonno Angelo's cremated ashes in his lap, and thought: *Well, Nonno Angelo, I took your advice, went to Sicily, reconnected with my family's roots, and learned of your youthful involvement with the Baron. Thank you, thank you, dear Nonno. Once again, I feel close to you, like in the old days when we were together in New Brunswick.*

Guy brushed away a tear, got up and replaced the container on the shelf. He had kept Nonno Angelo's ashes with him for almost twenty years now, always feeling a little guilty that he never arranged for their burial in the double plot in New Brunswick, next to Nonna Rosa. But his own need to feel Nonno Angelo was close-by, overrode these feelings of guilt. And now, after his trip, he felt even more *at one* with his grandfather. These thoughts reminded him of the Taormina album, so he went over and retrieved it from his luggage. He removed all the Brotherhood photos and found an empty stationery box to keep them in, for easier access in the future. It was only after he had spent a long time gazing at their images of Angelo, Rocco, Amadeo, Luca, Roberto and himself, that he remembered he needed to call Chad and let him know he got home safely, and to email Luca with the same message. Later, after he had called Chad and confirmed for Saturday and sent an email to Luca, he had a light meal thrown together from canned goods he'd left in the pantry two months earlier, briefly watched television until he was overwhelmed by the continual coverage of the War on Terror, and made an early night of it.

Guy woke up early the next morning rested, after having gone to bed so early the night before. He had some pressing shopping to do today – restocking his refrigerator and buying gifts to send Luca and his family, but the stores wouldn't be open yet. So, he passed the time unpacking his luggage while he used the TV remote to channel-surf. The war news was ubiquitous, from channel-to-channel: *Al-Qaeda..... War on Terror........ Afghanistan..... Taliban..... intense bombing...... war casualities.*

Before leaving his apartment, Guy checked his email and found a reply from Luca — grateful for his safe return home, wishing him good luck, and asking him to keep in frequent touch. He then decided to pay a visit to his Department Chairman at GWU, before shopping, so he took the Metro to Foggy Bottom and walked to campus. He found Will Davis in his office. After the customary greetings and queries about his trip, Davis asked about his book.

"It's coming along very nicely. I figure I have about five more chapters to write. Hopefully, I'll get them done this winter."

"Do you think you'll be interested in teaching in the Summer Term, or do you want to wait until the Fall Term?" Davis asked.

"If I finish the book by June, I'd probably want to teach, because that's when my Sabbatical pay ends. But, if I feel I just need a few more months of uninterrupted work on the book over the summer to be *completely* done, it would probably make more sense for me to live off savings during the summer in order to finish it *before* Fall Term begins."

"Yes, that makes sense. Well, let me know as soon as you can if you want a Summer Term contract. If not, we'll see you back on board in the Fall."

After he left Davis' office, Guy took the Metro to the Federal Triangle Station. Along Pennsylvania Avenue he found shops where he could purchase gifts for his Sicilian relatives. He bought Theresa tea towels and potholders, decorated with scenes of the District. For Luca, he found a beautiful photography book on the major monuments in town, and for the twins – who enjoyed sports, he purchased Washington Redskins items – caps, shirts.

On his ride back to the Cleveland Park Station, two blocks from his apartment, he realized he wouldn't be able to carry a lot of groceries along with these items, so when he exited the Station, he went across the street to the small mom-and-pop market and bought just enough fresh food to get him through the weekend. When he got home, he put the food away and quickly wrapped the gifts for Luca's family in a single box. He walked the several blocks to the Post Office down near the Metro station and mailed the package to Sicily, shortly before it closed for the day. Afterwards, he spent another quiet night channel-surfing on TV – skipping from one report of the 9/11 horror and the follow-up War on Terror to another while he ate dinner, and then went to bed early.

By Saturday afternoon, he was dressed and ready to follow the plan Chad proposed for his birthday. He was to meet Chad at the Lambda Rising gay bookstore on Dupont Circle at five. Guy took the Metro down to the Circle and walked over to the store a few minutes before five. Chad was nowhere in sight, so Guy went to the back of the store where the magazines were kept. Men were lined up three-deep, perusing the latest issues of *Honcho, Blueboy, Mandate* and the rest. It was crowded and awkward. One had to reach past people to return a magazine to the shelves and retrieve another – and there was no privacy. Guy studied his fellow "readers" out of the corner of his eye. There were two very elderly White gentlemen in the crowd, each with a young Black caregiver in attendance. One of these men stood upright holding onto a walker and unable to also hold a magazine, so his caregiver held it in front of his face and turned a page each time the elderly man nodded. More curious, however, was the other elderly gentleman, who was blind, and who stood next to his caregiver as the latter described the pictures to him:

"Black guy, big uncut dick, holding a baseball bat and smiling. Redheaded twink, tiny cock, shaved balls and cock, smoking a cigar." With each description, the older man became visibly excited and licked his lips.

A tap on the shoulder by Chad brought Guy out of his voyeurism. They quickly embraced, and exchanged greetings, remarking how well each of them looked after two months. Guy handed Chad a box holding the Italian silk ties, which the latter examined and "loved." He gave Guy a "thank-you" peck on the cheek. Then Chad said, "Okay, while I'm checking out the new crop of magazines, pick out a birthday gift – video, book, whatever."

"But," Guy replied, "dinner tonight is gift *enough*."

"No – only part of it. Now go pick out something!"

Guy wandered around the store, checking out the videos and "novelties", but nothing turned him on. So he went to the photography book display and settled on *Bruce of Los Angeles*, a book of male nudes by Bruce Bellas, a pioneer in such work. When he showed it to Chad at the checkout counter, Chad approved of his choice.

From Lambda Rising, they walked to a nearby restaurant for dinner. After a pleasant dinner, they went to Chad's parked car and drove to *The Hearth*, their favorite gay bar. Guy looked forward to seeing the old place again – so civilized, with a piano player discretely playing the standards of Cole Porter, Jerome Kern, Rodgers and Hart. *The Hearth* was one of the few gay bars left where one could have a quiet conversation across the table without having to shout over loud music.

As they entered the large room which resembled an English gentleman's club, with its dark paneling and Regency-style fireplace, Guy stopped in his tracks.

The beautiful grand piano was gone. In its place, in the heavily-draped and curtained bay window facing the street, was a stack of modern electronic equipment. One of the "old queens" who frequented the place was lifting a mike to his lips as he started a karaoke version of *Hello Dolly*.

Guy glanced at Chad, confused. "Yes," the latter said, anticipating his question, "Carl turned *The Hearth* into a karaoke bar while you were away. He said he had to do something to bring in more free-spending customers. Of course, he means a 'younger' crowd."

Guy followed Chad to their favorite table, in a mild state of shock. He automatically ordered white wine when the waiter arrived, and in seething silence watched one patron after another get up and imitate Merman, Garland and Streisand, accompanied by the karaoke track. Chad was well-aware of Guy's discomfort and suppressed anger, so he kept conversation to a minimum. When the "showgirls" tired of singing, three of them came over to the table and pulled up chairs without being invited. They professed to want to welcome Guy home from his trip. These three men were all in their late seventies, having spent their bachelor lives shuffling papers anonymously in the federal bureaucracy, and having survived the McCarthy-era witch-hunts by being heavily-closeted in those days. Now, in retirement, they spent their days in tiny efficiency apartments, emerging at night to openly cavort in gay bars, seeking young "meat" – no longer afraid of losing their careers or pensions. They dressed in out-of-style sports coats and suits, with bow ties. Collectively, they were known at *The Hearth* as "the aunties" – always ready to give motherly advice and sympathy – unless one was the current target of their gossip.

"My dear boy," one of them said to Guy, "hearts all over the District pined for you in your absence."

"Yes," another added, "and we understand some-one has a birthday tonight – may we pull down your pants and spank your little tushie?"

Comments like these flew around the table for several minutes, while Guy forced himself to appear good-natured and as if he were enjoying the atten-tion. Finally, one of the men – Cecil, said to Chad, "Have you told *him* about the *major* scandal during his absence?"

Chad responded, "You mean Weinstein?"

"Of course, Weinstein! Who else would I mean, Mary?"

Chad's face flushed a bit. Like Guy, he didn't care for swishy "Mary" talk, but he held his tongue.

Guy then interjected. "You mean Brian Weinstein, the psychotherapist?"

"Right, birthday-boy – the 'Analyst to Faggots, Extraordinaire'."

"What about him?"

"Well, my dear, it seems he's been 'keeping' a little thug twink, and they got into an argument in Weinstein's kitchen last month and the thug stabbed him in the shoulder with a sharp paring knife. He then took off with Weinstein's Porsche and one of his credit cards. Weinstein called a cab and got to the emergency room, but refused to press charges when the police were called in by hospital personnel. He canceled the credit card the next morning, but made no attempt to find the car or the twink. The worse part is, the story spread like wildfire around the gay community, and Weinstein – who's now very depressed, has closed his practice indefinitely and gone to stay at his condo in Aspen. Can you believe it, Mary? The shrink is depressed and his private life is apparently as screwed up as everyone else's!"

Guy nodded, and slightly smiled, relieved because someone had just started to sing *Over the Rainbow* at the karaoke station, so that everyone's attention was now diverted away from him and his table. *Well,* he thought, *that's one less headache for me.* Guy had been wondering how to tell Weinstein he wanted to suspend his therapy sessions, because he was no longer troubled by his failed personal relationships. How to do this without mentioning his newfound fulfillment in the Brotherhood would have been difficult. Now, with Weinstein's practice closed indefinitely – possibly forever, the issue was moot.

After the Garland imitator took several bows and sat down, Harry – another of the aunties, related his recent "abuse" from a newly-arrived Midwestern hustler – Storm. Harry had a pattern of over-indulging the District's fresh meat, until they got tired of him and deserted him for wealthier "johns". As soon as he finished his tired old story, Guy rolled his eyes in Chad's direction, and said, "I'm a bit tired, Chad, is it okay if we go?"

"Just a few minutes more, Guy. Let me go to the men's room first."

When Chad returned to the table, he was accompanied by a beautiful young cook's helper, carrying a birthday cake ablaze with forty candles. Most of the other patrons in the bar rushed over to the table and joined in the singing of *Happy Birthday*.

Guy blushed, less in embarrassment over the fuss being made than in the fact that the cake – with chocolate icing, was shaped like the huge fore-skinned penis of a Black man.

After the singing stopped and the candles were blown, the crowd entreated Guy to cut and eat the first piece. After a bit of thought, and knowing what *this* crowd wanted, Guy sliced off the chocolate fore-skinned tip, put it on a plate, and ate it in one swallow. The crowd went wild with applause. When Chad leaned over to give him a birthday kiss on the cheek, Guy whispered in his ear, "When in Rome....."

Later, as they pulled up to Guy's apartment building in Chad's car, Guy invited him up for a nightcap. Chad stammered a bit and then said, "Thanks, Guy, but I've got to get back to *The Hearth*. That hottie kitchen helper with the cake? He slipped me a note telling me what time he gets off work tonight. We'll probably wind up at my place. You now the score."

Guy laughed, as he exited the car and thanked Chad for this wonderful multi-stage birthday celebration. As he rode in the elevator up to his floor, he wondered how many other assignations were made at *The Hearth* tonight, how long they would last, and whether the endings would be tragic, as in the case of Brian Weinstein and his boy-toy.

· TWENTY ·

Early the following Tuesday, Guy took the Metro to Union Station and started the train journey which would eventually take him to his meeting in New Brunswick with Austin Walker, his Trust officer.

As with Dulles Airport less than a week earlier, Guy found security to be highly visible at Union Station. Armed guards were everywhere. Almost two months after 9/11, D.C. still had the appearance of an armed camp, under siege. And while at home, Guy reduced his television viewing significantly, as the litany of horror was endlessly played out: *Al Qaeda…..* *War on Terror….. enemy soldiers….. Afghan warlords…..* *Taliban….. body count.*

Once he settled into his seat on the train, he pulled out one of the professional art journals which had accumulated during his absence. He nervously scanned the book review section. Like most authors, he lived in fear that someone would publish a competing (or better) book before his own went to press. To date, a number of writers had published on male nude photography, but he continued to believe his approach to the subject was just different enough to warrant its own eventual distribution.

The journal and its contents kept him occupied – with his mind off the War on Terror, until he eventually arrived at the New Brunswick train station. He put the journal in the thin leatherette file folder he carried today, picked up his folding umbrella, and went directly to the taxi stand, outside the station.

Soon, he was at the trust office of Austin Walker, who had suggested a noon meeting, with a sandwich lunch ordered in from a nearby deli, to commemorate Guy's fortieth birthday, and to save time – since Guy planned to return to Washington later the same day.

Guy had previously talked with Walker on the phone and written correspondence had passed between them in recent years – since the previous gentleman handling Guy's affairs had retired. But this was the first time they'd met. Walker presented himself in a friendly manner, but with the pale, pasty complexion that comes from hours spent indoors, bent over balance sheets. He talked about Guy's estate in the hushed tones of a funeral director planning an interment.

"I see, Mr. Zambri – from my predecessor's notes, your grandfather died about twenty years ago."

"Yes."

"And the only requests for advances you made on the principal of the Trust were for college tuition and living expenses while you were a student – including health insurance coverage."

"Yes. That was all allowed under the terms of his Will. However, as soon as I started working, I never asked for any more advances."

"That's correct. Most of the correspondence in your file seems to be from your accountant."

"Yes. I have no real head for figures – or interest in the investment world. I've always led a simple life, and I've been more interested in stimulating my mind than in pursuing material things. I was more than happy to have my accountant analyze the correspondence I received from your firm, fill out the forms – including those for the income tax people, and then just give them to me to sign."

"I gathered that. Although it appears you did get involved about a decade ago when the previous trust officer suggested you let us sell the real estate and invest the proceeds."

"Yes. It was explained to me that a property management firm was being paid substantial sums to handle the tenant situation at both buildings. That they had to screen tenants, supervise them, collect rents, provide maintenance and repairs, keep up the taxes and insurance – all of which they happily billed to the Trust. I was also told the properties had appreciated substantially due to continuing inflation in the New Brunswick real estate market – thanks to the thousands of students at Rutgers, and that it was an ideal time to sell."

"It certainly was. You're aware that our agents were able to unload *both* properties in less than six months."

"I *was* surprised that they moved *that* quickly. Real estate has always appeared to me to be a millstone around one's neck. That's probably why I've always rented."

"Well, there are responsibilities to being a property owner – but there are also rewards. After the sales, we invested the proceeds in low-risk investments with modest returns, as you requested."

"Yes – I'm a 'bird-in-the-hand' kind of person. The high-risk stuff has the potential to pay greater dividends, but I didn't want to invest my time and energy in worrying about such things – as do so many of my friends and acquaintances."

"Well, after we sign these papers today, giving control of the Trust to you, you may decide to make some changes in your life. Perhaps even become a homeowner instead of a renter."

"I doubt it," Guy said with a small laugh.

At this point, Walker's secretary interrupted to bring in the lunch – deli sandwiches, potato salad, fruit Danish and iced tea. As they ate, Walker reviewed the transfer document.

"Now, we understand from our recent correspondence with you and your accountant that you want our firm to continue to handle the funds and invest them – under your direction, in keeping with the fee schedule we provided."

"Yes."

"And you still want the investments to be conservative and insured – despite the lower interest rates they offer?"

"Yes."

"All right, then. Why don't you read over the new document, which spells that all out, while I discuss my afternoon appointments with my secretary – and I'll be back shortly to answer any questions and show you where to sign it."

Walker left the room and Guy picked up the new Trust Agreement with his right hand, while he raised an apple Danish pastry to his lips with his left. On the bottom of the first page, the current value of the Trust leapt out at him and he almost dropped the pastry: *$310,000!*

Guy sat in disbelief. He couldn't believe Nonno Angelo's modest savings, and those two wood-frame buildings in the Italian ghetto of New Brunswick – purchased so many decades ago for less than $20,000

each, could have resulted in this legacy. He was glad
Austin Walker was out of the room and not there to
see the tears streaming down his face. Even twenty
years after his death, Nonno Angelo continued to
watch over him. First the bizarre Italian travel message delivered through Martin Francis earlier in the
summer, and now this!

By the time Walker returned, Guy had finished
reading the document, regained his composure, and
had written down several fundamental questions for
clarification.

"Your accountant has already reviewed the document through the mail – while you were abroad. Here
is a letter he sent, suggesting several small changes,"
Walker said, as he handled Guy a piece of paper.

Guy was gratified to see the issues his accountant
raised, as they were obviously in his best interests.
He was also grateful that he long-ago found an accountant who had also gone to law school – although
he never actively practiced the latter profession.

"Yes – I noticed those provisos in the text. I had a
couple minor questions – more for clarification than
anything else."

After Walker responded to the issues Guy raised,
the document was signed in several places, a copy
was made and given to Guy to put in his leatherette
file folder and take with him, and Austin Walker offered to mail another directly to Guy's accountant.
As he showed Guy to the door, Walker indicated that
his firm was delighted Guy had chosen to keep them
involved – since he had the option now of moving
the funds elsewhere, and that he looked forward to a
long, continuing relationship. Walker dryly joked that
at age forty, Guy was about to get his feet *directly* wet
in the world of investments, and would likely find

himself much more actively involved in such matters in the future than he had ever imagined. Guy laughed, in return, made a polite, non-committal response and found his way out of the building and onto the street. His wristwatch indicated it was a quarter past one in the afternoon. He stood on the curb a few minutes until he hailed a cab, which he directed to take him to his old neighborhood. He didn't anticipate being in New Brunswick again for some time to come – maybe never again, so he decided to visit some of the old haunts this afternoon.

Guy had the cab driver drop him off on the street where Nonno Angelo's apartment building was located. He walked half a block to a bus stop across from the building and sat on the bench, in order not to appear conspicuous, since there were a number of young children playing on the sidewalk, and several adults gathered on porches and steps, talking.

The building was unchanged, except for the color. Nonno Angelo loved beige paint, with dark brown trim, and both his properties had been so painted. Now, however, the building was hunter green, with white trim. Long porches ran across the front of the building, on both the first and second floors. As Guy looked at the large door in the middle of the first-floor porch, he remembered the many times he had accompanied Nonno Angelo here to collect the rents. On the other side of the door – unless there had been renovations, was a large hall with a door on the right and another on the left – leading to the first-floor apartments, and a stairway going up to the second floor, where the apartment configuration was the same. Each of the apartments had two bedrooms and one bath.

On the rent-collecting trips, Guy became familiar with almost every possible excuse someone might have for not paying his bills. Each month, at least one of the four tenants asked for a delay on the rent payment, or claimed ability to only pay part of the amount due. Nonno Angelo listened to each story, and was fair and patient – for which he paid a price when he delivered the incomplete revenue to Nonna Rosa. "Chicken-hearted," she would say, "You're chicken-hearted!" Occasionally, even his patience and trust wore thin and he would have to ask someone to move, due to chronic non-payment of rent. As a child, Guy could never understand why the "deadbeats" acted as if *they* were the victims – cursing poor Nonno Angelo as they loaded their belongings onto vehicles.

But that was long ago and now, as Guy studied the people coming in and out of the building and congregating on the porch and stairs, he realized this neighborhood was no longer an Italian-American bastion. Not only were there several people of color around – as well as multi-racial children, but also some women dressed in very exotic Middle-Eastern and Far-Eastern garb.

Well, he thought, *that's enough here. Let me walk down to the store and our old apartment.*

Guy walked the two blocks to his old address, but when he was several doors away, he decided the building must have been torn down and replaced, because he couldn't spot it. Finally, after recognizing the buildings which would have been on either side of his old home, he realized the garish, aqua-blue building, with a white aluminum awning over the large window which once served as the grocery's store's distinguishing feature, was in fact Nonno Angelo's old place. When he looked up to the second-floor apartment, he noticed that the living-room windows were also topped with white aluminum awnings.

Guy stared at the large storefront window. Where small neon signs once hung advertising beer, soda and ice cream, there now was a large bright-pink neon sign proclaiming: *Vito's House of Beauty.*

After he had absorbed the garish transformation of this once-staid little building, he walked up to the window and tried to peek inside. He was curious to see if anything inside resembled the old store. A hair stylist, in a pink smock, was working on a woman seated near the window, and she looked up at Guy as he stared in. Her expression was one of puzzlement at this stranger "peeking" in the window. Guy was too preoccupied to be concerned about this, but she wasn't. She put down her scissors and comb and walked to the door. She opened it a few inches and said, "May I help you?"

Guy was suddenly embarrassed, and muttered, "Uh, no."

She looked at him suspiciously. "Are you here to pick someone up?"

"Uh, no.....I.....I used to live here years ago. Actually — upstairs. My grandfather's grocery store was down here. I haven't been back to New Brunswick in years and don't know when I'll be back again, so I just wanted to see if the place was still here."

"Oh," she replied, loosening her grip on the door. "Why don't you come in and look around?"

Guy eagerly accepted her invitation. As he entered, he noticed the name tag – *Cleo*, pinned on her smock.

There were only two customers at the moment – the one Cleo was working on and another sitting under a hair dryer. Guy didn't recognize either of them, and they didn't seem to recognize him.

"So, you used to live upstairs?" Cleo asked, as she cut hair.

"Yes – and work down here."

"Huh. You know, Vito the owner is in the backroom sorting inventory. He was raised in this neighborhood. Maybe he knew your family." Before Guy could respond, she called out, "Vito, Vito – come out here," in a very unattractive, loud voice. *Somehow*, Guy thought, *her loud voice goes with her overly-made-up face and large mass of overly-teased hair.*

A minute or so later, a middle-aged man emerged from the backroom and walked toward them. He wore an aqua-colored barber's smock. The shirt underneath was opened halfway down his chest, and from his neck hung multiple gold chains. On one wrist was a gold watch, and on the other a gold identification bracelet. There were several gold rings on the fingers of each hand. On his head was an undoubtedly expensive, but nevertheless *obvious*, hairpiece.

"Hey, Vito," Cleo said in a thick Jersey accent, "this guy says he used to live upstairs. His grandfather had a store down here."

Vito looked at Guy and said, "Zambri? Why you're Guy Zambri!"

"Vito? Vito Aligeri?" Guy replied, as he extended his hand in greeting.

"Well, I'll be damned! What are you doing *here*, Guy?"

"I had to come to New Brunswick on important business today, and decided to take a quick look around the old neighborhood before I catch my train back to Washington."

Vito Aligeri seemed genuinely pleased to see Guy. He took him by the arm and said, "Come on in the backroom – there's a coffee machine and a place where we can sit down and talk."

The "backroom" turned out to be a combination staff lounge and storage area. Against one wall was a large pink vinyl-covered couch. On the opposite wall were shelves stocked with beauty supplies. A small table was in one corner. On it sat a coffee maker which Vito turned on, and a box of *Dunkin Donuts* — obviously leftover from this morning. An open door on the back wall indicated a powder room for staff and customers. After Vito poured a cup of the re-heated coffee for Guy, and handed it to him, he said, "Want a donut?"

"No thanks – I just had lunch less than an hour ago. So, how long have you been here? I didn't know you bought this place from my grandfather's estate."

"I didn't. Some other guy did – but after just a year or two, his marriage fell apart and they had to divide up their assets, so I got a good price. They both wanted out of the situation in a hurry, so it was a buyer's market."

"The last time I saw you, it was on your wedding day."

"Really? Were you invited? We had such a *small* wedding, hardly anyone was invited."

"No, I wasn't invited. I just happened to be passing the parish church – on the other side of the street, on my way to the movies — and saw you and Tina come out, with people throwing rice."

"Yeah, that was just the immediate family."

"Then, a few days later, the wedding announcement was in the local paper and said you were moving to Newark."

"Yeah – we stayed there almost eight years. The girls – I have two, were born there, I went to beauty culture school, and then worked for a string of nasty bastards."

"What made you come back to New Brunswick?"

"Tina – actually her old lady got sick. We needed to be closer. I got work here, and then the old lady died and left us the money that I used to buy this place."

"Well, you certainly have transformed it. I'm having trouble placing the old shelves that held the canned goods, or the fresh-meat case, in my mind's eye."

"The plumbing and electrical were the biggest jobs – and biggest expense. You know — all these sinks and electrical outlets. But it worked out. Anyway, what about you? You're in Washington now?"

"Yes – I've been there since I graduated from Rutgers. First for graduate school at George Washington University, and then I just stayed on to teach."

"Would you believe my two daughters are both at Rutgers? Vito Aligeri's kids in college?"

"Congratulations! Do you all live upstairs?"

"Yeah, and are we crowded!"

"I guess the girls have to share my old room."

"And *that* has been a nightmare! But, I can't afford to have them stay in the dorms on campus. Anyway, the older one graduates in June and insists she's getting her own place then, and then the younger one will have the room to herself for her last two years in college. But, what about *you*? Married? Divorced? Kids?"

"No – I've stayed single. Married to my job, I guess."

"Ah, you bachelors – all that pussy every night! Am I right?"

Guy had a standard answer for this oft-raised question among *the boys* – "I get my fair share," he said, with a smirk.

"Well," Vito said, "let me tell you — a place like *this* is 'pussy-heaven'. First, you got the workers. They come and go, but most of them will do *anything* to get a job and keep it. My cock gets sucked so much, it's a wonder it doesn't fall off! Ha! Ha!"

"Do you just have Cleo on staff?"

"No – there's another girl, Annie. She's not in today. Every month when she's got the rag on, she's out. She's a frigid bitch. Now Cleo – what a mouth on her! Ha! Ha!"

Guy took a swig from his coffee mug while Vito continued. "You know, I see bare titty *every* day. These broads don't wear bras anymore. So, I tell them they got to unbutton while I place the towel around their necks for shampooing, and then I see an eyeful! Most of them feel ignored by their husbands, so they encourage me to cop a feel, here and there. And then, the most neglected ones eventually come right out and ask me to screw them after hours. I send Cleo and Annie home, tell Tina I'll be upstairs a little later because I've got inventory or bookwork – or I just wait for her to go somewhere, and I bring the cunts back here. You see this couch we're sitting on – it's a fuck-mobile! You wouldn't believe the action I've had on this thing. See that locked cabinet over there? I'm the only one with a key. I keep a box with a gross of rubbers in there. Well, it started out as a *gross*! Ha! Ha!"

By now, Guy decided that he had seen and heard enough, so he made a point of holding up his wrist-watch and saying, "Look at the time. I've got to get back to the station to catch my train home. Can I use your phone to call a cab, Vito?"

"Of course. Come with me. I even have a taxi number handy. We use the same outfit all the time – my cousin runs it."

About ten minutes later, Guy shook hands with Vito, thanked him for his hospitality, and climbed into the back seat of the waiting cab. As he waved goodbye through the window, he directed the driver to the station.

Once the train left the station, and he was free to contemplate the day's events, Guy first thought of his legacy: *Over $300,000! I can't believe it!* The mere thought of it was over-whelming, and he decided to put it out of his mind until the next day. Tonight, if he got home early enough, he'd call Chad and give him the news. If not, it could wait another day. In any event, he'd take a non-prescription sleeping tablet as soon as he got home, to ensure he didn't toss and turn all night with visions of dollar signs in his head.

The unexpected encounter with Vito Aligeri today would provide enough rumination for his active mind on the train trip ahead. As the scenery sped swiftly by the window, next to his seat, he was taken back to a quiet Sunday morning about thirty years ago, when a life-changing event happened to him – with no advanced warning.

As a child helping in his grandparents' store, Guy came to know – or at least recognize, most of the people in the neighborhood. In the case of older boys, like Vito Aligeri, Guy only had a nodding acquaintance with them. Vito was three years older, so they never were in class together – either in the public school or in catechism classes at church. Thus, he had no reason to anticipate the events of that long-ago Sunday morning – when he was eleven years old and heard Vito call out his name and run to catch up with him on his way home from the Children's Mass. After he made his First Communion, his grandparents allowed him to go to church alone most Sundays – to the nine o'clock Children's Mass. They preferred the seven o'clock "old peoples' mass", favored by old-timers who rose very early out of lifelong habit and wanted to get home and take care of other matters. In the case of Nonno Angelo, it was to read the Sunday papers and work on his accounts from the store. For Nonna Rosa, Sunday morning was spent giving her homemade pasta sauce (begun on Saturday) several *more* hours of simmering on the stove before the traditional Sunday dinner between twelve-thirty and one. Guy's routine after church, was to read the Sunday comics and selected items in the rest of the paper, watch TV, and hope to go to the neighborhood movies in the afternoon. – usually by himself, but sometimes with one or both of his grandparents.

On this particular Sunday, as the fourteen-year-old Vito caught up with Guy on the sidewalk, he said, "Hey, Zambri – I saw your grandfather's new wagon. Sharp!"

Guy felt a bit of pride in the new burgundy station wagon Nonno Angelo had recently purchased. As he told Guy, "We can use it as a family car for the three of us, and I can still make home deliveries to customers and haul stock from the wholesaler — by folding down the back seat and making extra room."

Guy proudly responded to Vito, flattered by this unexpected attention from one of the "big guys" in the neighborhood, "Yeah, it's cool."

As they walked along, Vito lavished praise on the wagon and then asked what the interior was like. "Is it burgundy too?"

"No, it's gray leather – well, not *real* leather."

"Sounds nice. Could I look at it? Is your grandfather home?"

"He should be. The wagon should be in the driveway or garage."

When they reached Guy's driveway, it was empty. Pointing to the detached garage at the far end, he said, "It's in there. Come on – my grandfather keeps the side door to the garage unlocked during the day."

As soon as they entered the garage, Guy went to the driver's side and Vito to the passenger's side. After Guy settled behind the steering wheel and Vito sat next to him, they began to admire the interior of the wagon – commenting on the buttons, knobs and upholstery. The vehicle still had that "new car smell", which prompted a discussion of the various vehicles their respective families had owned over the years, and how much longer each had to wait until he could drive a car. Guy was especially envious that Vito would be getting a driver's learning permit long before he would.

At some point in the conversation, Guy became aware that it had shifted, but he didn't know where it was going. Vito was saying strange things, using unfamiliar words he didn't recognize. Finally, he swallowed his pride and risked appearing to be an "ignorant little jerk", and said to Vito, "I don't understand what you're talking about."

Vito sighed, smiled at Guy in a patronizing way, and said, "I was asking how often you jerk-off – you know – beat off, pound off?"

207

"Uh," Guy stammered, "I don't know what that is."

"Ah," Vito replied. "Well, it's something only big boys do. If you think you're ready to be a big boy, I'll show you."

Guy assumed Vito was talking about some kind of athletic skill involving a ball, and said, "Okay – there are some balls on the shelf over there. Which one do we need?"

Vito laughed out loud. "You need *two*, kid – and you've got them both in the front seat! Here, look." With that, Vito unzipped his fly, and took out his penis. Guy was as much shocked at this unexpected action as he was over the fact that Vito's "big-boy" pee-pee was no larger than his own.

Vito started to stroke it slowly. "See, you stroke it and it gets bigger. And it feels *so* good. Try it."

Guy was mesmerized by this "big-boy" secret, and slowly removed his own pale penis from his pants and began to imitate Vito.

"Isn't it good?" Vito asked, after a few minutes.

"Oh, yes," Guy replied. "It's fun, isn't it?"

Suddenly, Vito started to moan and throw his body back and forth in jerky spasms. Then, to Guy's amazement, a thick white liquid shot out of Vito's penis. Luckily, Vito had his handkerchief ready to catch it, so the new interior of the station wagon wasn't soiled. Vito continued to "milk" his organ for some time before he said, "Ah, that was good," and wiped it off one more time with the handkerchief and then put it back in his trousers.

Guy automatically stopped stroking, but Vito said, "No. Go on. You haven't 'cum' yet."

"Cum?"

"You know — that white stuff. Don't be afraid."

Since Vito didn't appear hurt in any way, Guy continued until he felt a series of spasms in his organ, and tingling in his testicles. Finally, there was a rush of pleasure through his genitals and he moaned like Vito had a bit earlier. When he looked down at his lap, there was no "white stuff".

"Where is it? What happened, Vito?"

"Nothing bad. You usually don't cum the first few times. It takes awhile. Just keep practicing. In a week or two, it should happen. Always have a hankie or tissue ready. Let me know when you start to cum and then we'll talk some more. See you kid."

With that, Vito Aligeri exited the station wagon, left the garage, went down the driveway and disappeared around the corner of Nonno Angelo's store.

Guy sat behind the steering wheel for a while, trying to compose himself before going into the house. He wasn't *really* sure what had just happened, but he knew it was *wonderful*!

For the next two weeks, he "practiced" every day, and eventually started to get the sought-after discharge. A few days after his first ejaculation, he ran into Vito at the movies and whispered to him that he was cumming. Vito suggested they meet in Nonno Angelo's garage after Mass the following Sunday, to discuss the matter. And thus began a wonderful idyll, lasting over one and one-half years, during which Guy and Vito met once or twice a week, for sexual exploration and mutual pleasure. They expanded the setting to include their respective apartments, Vito's family's garage, the nearby park – and even the basement hall of the parish church! Wherever and whenever the opportunity arose, they went at it like the sex-driven

ephebes they were. As time passed, Vito introduced
Guy to more pleasurable pastimes. However, Guy
drew the line at *penetration*. His fear of being entered
by another man started with Vito, who had to content himself with awkward, simulated intercourse –
slowly rubbing himself against Guy's back, while he
whispered over and over in Guy's ear, "I'm pretending you're a girl, I'm pretending you're a girl."

Guy's life became very full and satisfying. Schoolwork, helping in the store, and secretly meeting with
Vito as often as possible consumed him until that
day almost two years later when he realized Vito was
avoiding him. It started with Vito's chronic excuses
as to why he couldn't meet Guy for assignations.
Then, he started ignoring Guy when they passed each
other on the street, at church, or when he came into
the store to buy something. The dawn came for Guy
one Sunday morning when he emerged from the
Children's Mass to find Vito walking off with Tina
Albanese. Guy secretly followed them at a distance
until he saw them turn down Vito's parents' driveway. They glanced around nervously, to see if anyone
were watching, and then headed for Vito's father's
garage.

Guy was crushed! He thought of the dozens of
times he and Vito had pleasured each other in that
place – and now he had been rejected for a new "play-
mate".

Guy rushed home, went to his room to await Sunday dinner, and had a good cry. He had never felt
abandoned by his parents, because they were out of
his life when he was just an infant – and his grandparents more than made up for his unfortunate start
in life. But in Vito's case, he felt truly and completely

abandoned and betrayed.

For the next couple years, Vito and Guy avoided eye contact with each other when they came face-to-face in the neighborhood. Most of the time, Tina was with Vito, so there was *no* chance of discussing the matter. Then, one day right after Vito and Tina graduated from high school, Guy stumbled upon their wedding, on his way to the movies.

A few days later, he was stocking some of the lower shelves behind one of the glass cases in the store when he overheard a hushed conversation between several of the leading neighborhood gossips and Nonna Rosa. Guy had learned over the years to listen-in on the neighborhood gossips, who visited the store daily and exchanged "news" with his grandparents. On this day, they were discussing the brief announcement in the paper about the Aligeri-Albanese wedding. It soon became apparent to Guy that they were saying Tina was pregnant – and *that* was the reason for the hastily-arranged, small wedding *and* the move to Newark. It was assumed that one day they would visit New Brunswick with their child and lie about its age, and no one there would be the wiser.

But not too many months later, Guy overheard an update from Nonna's friends: Tina had miscarried.

While Guy stretched his arms in anticipation of exiting the train shortly, as it pulled into Union Station, he filled in the rest of the story from Vito's words earlier in the day. He and Tina apparently stayed in Newark for a total of eight years, had two *additional* successful pregnancies there, and *then* moved back to New Brunswick.

When he reached his apartment, he decided to wait until morning to tell Chad of his good fortune. He also decided not to take a sleeping pill – because it occurred to him that he had another way of falling asleep quickly, without one. He took a long shower, and then lay naked on his bed, and conjured up *every* memory he still had of his times spent in secret with Vito. As he jerked off to these memories, he celebrated the joy they brought him so long ago, and told himself he was finally exorcising the ghost of Vito Aligeri – who had hurt him deeply, and yet had introduced him to the wonder of self-love. For that, he would always be grateful.

• TWENTY-ONE •

As soon as Guy felt the plane rushing down the runway for take-off, he instinctively touched his seat belt. It was secured. Upon lift-off, he closed his eyes and luxuriated in his wide, comfortable Business Class seat. He had always flown in Coach in the past, in order to save money, but he always felt cramped and uncomfortable there. In addition, he experienced humiliation as a Coach Class passenger after a gay airline steward he met at one of Chad's parties told him cabin crews refer to Coach as the "cattle car", and its passengers as "cattle". Today, though, for the first time in his life, he was treating himself to the comfort and luxury of the Business Class cabin. Luckily, the seat next to him was unoccupied, so after the plane leveled off above the clouds, he planned to raise the arm rests between the two seats and spread out even more. The plane was flying with many empty seats, way below capacity. Even four months after 9/11 – it was now mid-January 2002, many people were still terrified of flying, and the airline industry was in serious trouble.

After the plane leveled off, and while the cabin attendants started to prepare appetizers and drinks for serving, Guy stared out the window, still trying to comprehend everything that had happened since he returned home in early November. A few days after he met with Austin Walker in New Brunswick and shared his good news with Chad, he suddenly seized upon a "wild" idea – to buy the apartment he had rented in Taormina. He ran the notion past his accountant and Walker – neither of whom had major objections, until Guy told them he wanted to pay cash. Both of them were of the persuasion that one takes out the largest mortgage possible, for the longest period of time, with the smallest down-payment – in order to conserve one's capital. But Guy insisted – as he was now in control of his inheritance, that he did not want to spend the rest of his life worrying about mortgage payments – and thus, would only buy real estate on a cash basis, even if it greatly reduced his capital. For their parts, Austin Walker and the accountant told Guy their responsibility ended with giving him their best professional advice, which he could take or leave. Once it was clear to Guy that he wanted to explore the matter further, he called Tonio Valli in Taormina.

"Tonio? Guy Zambri here."

"Guy – yes. How are you? Did you have a pleasant trip home?"

"Yes – it was without incident. And, shortly after I returned, I received an inheritance on my fortieth birthday. That's actually why I'm calling you. Have you sold the apartment I rented from you?"

"No – but I've discussed the situation with the owners in Belgium and we've set a price."

"What is it?"

"They're asking $150,000 in U.S. dollars. Why do you ask?"

"I want to buy it, Tonio – cash."

"Are you serious?"

"Yes – I have enough money from my inheritance, and am anxious to get back to Taormina while I'm still on sabbatical leave. A cash deal should expedite the sale, shouldn't it? I mean, no time tied up in mortgage processing, credit-rating checks, and so forth?"

"That's very true. But are you *sure* this is what you want to do?"

"Tonio, I'm surer of this than of any other decision I've ever made in my life. Do you think the owners would consider a lower offer?"

"You have the right to make an offer, and they have the right to accept, refuse or make a counter-offer. What do you propose?"

"Could I offer $145,000 and see what happens?"

"Of course. By the way, it will be in move-in condition by the time you close on it. I've inspected the unit with an employee of mine and we agreed the faucets on the sinks should be changed, as you suggested. I also have a larger refrigerator on order."

"Wonderful! That small one bugged me."

"The only other thing we decided to do prior to listing it for sale is to repaint it. Painters are actually scheduled for next week."

"It sounds perfect! So, what do *I* do to start this?"

"I'll draw up an offer from you to the sellers. I know you have email – I have your address on file from when you rented the unit. Do you also have fax?"

"No – but my accountant does. You can send everything there. I'll email you his fax number as soon as I get off the phone and look it up in my files. I'll also send you his name, address, phone number and so forth – for future reference."

"Okay – I'll then send the offer document for you to sign and fax back. If you make any changes, initial *each* change. After the sellers respond and we settle on a price and closing date, I'll fax a contract. At that point, you'll have to wire earnest money to validate the contract, but it will eventually be applied to the purchase price."

"That sounds good. So, we agree a cash deal should expedite matters. But, what about the Italian government – residency requirements and that kind of thing?"

"Well, you're not moving here permanently, are you? It's just a vacation home – right?"

"Yes. After my sabbatical leave I expect my pattern of occupancy will be to spend the summers there, a couple weeks at Christmas, and maybe a week or so during the University's Spring Break – which is usually in March."

"Good. Well, if you aren't trying to seek full-time residence we can avoid the bureaucratic nightmare of trying to obtain a *permesso di soggiorno* – which allows you to stay up to five years, or the *carta di soggiorno* – which is for permanent residency. However, there are various documents which will still have to be obtained in order for you to purchase property in Italy, as a foreigner. I am very familiar with the process, because I sell so much real estate to non-Italians. However, the Italian bureaucracy is among the world's worst – and most corrupt, so we will have to pay bribes in various places if you want to move this along quickly."

"How much in bribes?"

"I'd say about two-thousand American dollars. I'll take care of all of that, and afterwards you can reimburse me in private – and in secret. The Italian bureaucracy *cannot* function without bribery, but at the same time, considers it illegal, and one can be prosecuted for giving *or* receiving." Tonio said, with a loud laugh.

"Gosh,Tonio, I don't want you to get into any trouble."

"Not at all. I couldn't run my businesses without paying bribes left and right. I know what needs to be done and how to do it. Don't worry – leave it all to me. Do you have any other questions before I ring off to work up your offer document?"

"Yes – with no mortgage on the place, my expenses will be essentially limited to maintenance and taxes. Since the unit will be unoccupied for about eight months out of the year, could your firm handle the rental situation for me when I'm not using it myself?"

"Of course – we do that all the time, for a fee, naturally. However, if the unit will be available for rental eight months each year, you should be able to cover *all* your expenses through the rent, and also make a modest profit."

"It sounds good. I'll let you go now so you can get things started, and I'll look up the information on my accountant and email it right out to you."

"Arrivederci, then, Guy. It will be great having you back in Taormina!"

"I look forward to it, Tonio. Arrivederci!"

Within a week of that phone call, the Belgian sellers made a counter-offer of $146,500 – which Guy accepted. After that, documents and funds flowed back and forth between America and Sicily, and despite the reluctant assistance and ignored advice of his accountant and Austin Walker, Guy was now on his way to take possession of his apartment at the Villa Paradiso – and hopefully finish his book by the start of Fall Semester at GWU. His laptop, reference books, and partially-completed manuscript were all on board the flight, along with the metal container filled with Nonno Angelo's cremated ashes. Tomorrow, after his connecting flight from Rome to Palermo, Guy would be met by Luca at the airport. On the drive to Taormina, they would stop in Messina and go to the harbor from which Nonno Angelo had sailed to America so many years ago. There, Guy would distribute some of the ashes in the water. Later, after he was settled in his apartment in Taormina, Luca would take him to Pietro Stanza's farm, where Guy would distribute more of his grandfather's ashes in the grove where Angelo had posed for the Baron. Then, Guy and Luca would go down to the beach, below the cliffs of Taormina – where Nonno Angelo, his brother Rocco, and their father Amadeo fished in the sea. There, the rest of the ashes would be dispersed.

Yes, Guy thought, as he settled back in his seat and listened to Andrea Bocelli on his headset, *Nonno Angelo, the Sicilian Prince, is crossing the vast ocean one last time and going home – forever.*

THE END

CPSIA information can be obtained at www.ICGtesting.com
Printed in the USA
BVOW04s1816291014

372876BV00001B/5/P

9 781592 991501